THE MYSTERY OF
DOLPHIN INLET

THE MYSTERY OF
DOLPHIN
INLET

BY JAMES HOLDING

THE MACMILLAN COMPANY, NEW YORK

The Macmillan Company, New York
Collier-Macmillan Canada, Ltd., Toronto, Ontario
Library of Congress catalog card number: 68-11001
Printed in the United States of America
FIRST PRINTING

For that tireless fisherman, my son

CONTENTS

THE MYSTERY OF
DOLPHIN INLET

1 ⚡

AN AFTERNOON SWIM

The knife went in sweet and easy. Its point was like a needle and its edge like a razor. Without a pause or a hitch, it swept down smoothly against the backbone the full length, and sliced out free an inch from the end. Then, tight up against the tough skin, sawing back and forth with a little rocking motion, it came back again.

Behind me, a voice said, "How beautiful!" A girl's voice.

I looked over my right shoulder in surprise. "It's just a Spanish mackerel," I said. "Nothing beautiful about that." I flipped the fillet to one side and turned the fish over to cut out the other one.

"Well, *I* think there is," she said. She didn't move, just stood there behind me at the cleaning table by the tubs, watching me. "The way you're cleaning it."

I didn't turn my head. "I'm filleting it," I said.

"Whatever it is, I think it's beautiful, in a way. I mean your economy of *motion*. The way you know exactly where to cut and how, don't you see?"

How about that? I'm filleting a three-pound Spanish

mackerel for Mrs. Ferguson, and it's beautiful! It was a new angle. I'd never heard that one before.

"It's all in the knife," I said to her self-consciously. "If your knife's sharp enough, there's nothing to it."

I must have sounded sharp myself, or nervous at least, because out of the corner of my eye, I saw my sister Gloria, behind our display case, giving me one of those looks of hers that says, just as plain as words could say it: Relax, now, Pete, even if she's a girl. She won't bite you. I can't wait on her till I finish with Mrs. Ferguson.

That's quite a lot to put into one look but my sister Gloria can do it easy. She does it all the time. Because she knows that as much as I like girls—and I like them a lot— they make me kind of nervous. The minute I get alone with one, no matter how nice she is or how well I know her, I kind of tighten up and begin to act slightly like a jerk. Girls make me feel awkward and ugly, and I get this uneasy feeling that they may be laughing at me, you know what I mean? Anyway, it sometimes makes me sort of abrupt and grouchy-sounding when I don't mean it at all, when all I want is to be natural and cool like the other guys at school are with girls.

Gloria says I'm shy, that's all, but there's more to it than that. I guess if I was a girl and was looking around for a boy to date, I wouldn't pick out a guy like me. And you know why? Because I *am* pretty awkward and ugly, to tell the truth. And what's more, I smell of fish all the time.

Gloria argues with me about it a lot. She claims I'm awkward, maybe, but only socially, not physically. Only when I'm around girls and can't force myself to give out with a

lot of gushy sweet talk. She points out that I'm not awkward at all when it comes to diving, swimming, fishing,
cleaning fish and stuff like that. Only she never said I had
economy of motion, either!

So maybe I'm not really awkward, but there's no doubt
about my being ugly. Even Gloria can't argue away this
jagged scar across the side of my face that makes my cheek
look like a streak of white lightning had landed on it and
stayed there. When I was twelve, Pop took me out on the
Gulf in his boat one day, and I was fooling around with
a weighted hand line, leaning over the side and hauling up
fast, just for practice, when I jerked the line too hard and
it came shooting up at me out of the water like a rocket—
I still dream about it sometimes—and the hook went into
my cheek under my left eye. The backlash of the sinker
pulled the hook through my cheek and almost tore it in
half, clear down to my ear lobe. It was a real mess. Pop got
the hook out, but we couldn't get the tear cleaned up and
stitched until maybe four hours later when Pop finally got
his boat in off the Gulf through a squall that hit us. So the
scar isn't very pretty.

Oh, I'm ugly, all right, whatever Gloria says about my
being nearly six feet tall with the right muscles in the right
places and sun-bleached hair and friendly eyes. Without my
scar, maybe I'd be halfway decent-looking—like Mike Sebastien, the Perdido Key policeman who's always hanging
around our place courting Gloria. But with this scar, I'm
a seventeen-year-old monster, that's all. Face it.

And I smell of fish all the time, like I said. It's true. I do.
Because my father works this commercial fishing boat, fish-

ing the Gulf. He sells most of his catch to the wholesaler in Sarta City, and what's left he sells at retail in a little fish market he built right in front of our old house here on the bay side of Perdido Key, just east of Fiesta Village. My mother died a long time ago, but Gloria, my older sister— she's nineteen—she takes care of the fish market while Pop does the fishing. After school and during vacations I help Gloria out in the fish market, cleaning and filleting the fish she sells, packing in the ice for our display case and, now that I have a driver's license, delivering fish in our old pickup truck to our customers up and down the Key who order by phone or leave standing orders. Sometimes, for a treat, Pop lets me go out with him and his crew on the Gulf for a day or a night with the nets. One time last year, just before Christmas, I went out with him and we brought in over eight thousand pounds of mullet! That's a lot of fish. The wholesaler took the eight thousand pounds and there was enough left over to keep our smokehouse going for days. Folks down our way like smoked mullet better than candy bars.

I love to go out with Pop but the hours a commercial fisherman works are murder when you're a kid going to high school. So I spend most of my free time helping Gloria at the fish market. When I finish high school, though, my idea is to go to the university and get smartened up on navigation and oceanography and stuff like that, and then, with Pop as a partner, get hold of a modern shrimper and make a career out of commercial fishing. You can make a bundle that way if you go at it right.

Anyway, you can see why I smell of fish most of the time. No matter how often you wash, shower or swim, if you're working with fresh-caught fish a lot, it's hard to get rid of the smell.

I took another quick peek over my shoulder—the left one this time, so I showed my scar—at this girl my sister Gloria wanted me to be polite to, and I must admit she wasn't bad-looking. She had dark-brown hair, natural color, and blue eyes with long lashes and the top of her head came to about shoulder height on me. She hadn't spent much time in our South Florida sunshine lately because she had on cut-off blue jeans and a short-sleeved blouse and her bare legs and arms were an indoor white color. But nice.

She was smiling at me. When she smiled, she opened her eyes wide and one corner of her mouth went up higher than the other, kind of lopsided. But nice, you know? "With the sharpest knife in the world, *I* couldn't do what you're doing," she said. "I can paint pictures with a palette knife, but I can't fillet a fish. Do you mind my watching you?"

"Go ahead," I said, thinking to myself she had a nice voice, too, and she ought to weigh out at about a hundred pounds on the fish scales. She looked to be about sixteen or seventeen, I figured.

I finished with the mackerel and gave the fillets to Gloria to wrap up for Mrs. Ferguson, who was looking in her purse for money. While I ran water from the spigot over my hands and wiped off the cleaning table, I said to the girl, "You're not from around here, are you?"

"No, I'm a tourist," she said. "My mother and I are staying up at the Freebooter in a housekeeping cottage for ten days before Easter." The Freebooter is about the only big tourist place we've got on Perdido Key. It's a deluxe four-star restaurant at the north end of the Key on a nice beach with a cottage colony around it.

"We're doing our own cooking, mostly, and the Freebooter manager told us this is the best place to buy fish," the girl explained. She tossed her head back with a little sideways motion and her hair swung around behind her shoulder. It was a habit she had, I noticed later. "Mother's waiting outside in the car."

Gloria finished wrapping up Mrs. Ferguson's fish and took the money for it and rang it up on the cash register. She was ready to wait on the girl. I said, "Where do you live?"

"Tallahassee. My father's a lawyer. He's coming to join us here in a few days." She laughed. It was a nice hearty laugh, not a giggle. "*He's* really the one who needs the rest, not Mother and me."

"He'll get plenty of rest on Perdido Key, all right," I said. "It's pretty dead around here."

She didn't offer any comment on that, but drifted over toward Gloria and said, "This is Hobbs's Fish Market, so I guess your name must be Hobbs."

I didn't know whether she was talking to me or Gloria so I didn't say anything. Gloria said, "Yes, his name is Hobbs, and so is mine. He's Pete and I'm Gloria, and what can I do for you?"

"Do you have any shrimp?" the girl asked.

"Yes, very nice. Dollar fifty a pound green, and a dollar seventy-five cooked and cleaned."

"I'd like a pound cooked and cleaned, please. And a couple of fillets of that kind of fish Pete was just fixing." The girl used my name as naturally as if she'd known me all her life.

"Mackerel?" Gloria said. "Okay. I'll have to deliver the shrimp to you though if you want it cooked and cleaned. There's none ready right now. Did you say you were at the Freebooter?"

"Cottage twelve," the girl said.

"We'll deliver the fish and shrimp this afternoon, then, if that's all right?"

"Of course. Our name's Frost. I'm Susan Frost."

"Pete'll deliver it," Gloria said with a sidelong look at me. She wants everybody to have a romance. She's always trying to work it so I'll fall for somebody she thinks is my type. I guess she'd already decided that this Susan Frost qualified for e, and this time, I was all for it. "Pete drives our truck," Gloria went on while she rang up Susan's money on the register and made change. "He's old enough to have a driver's license now, isn't that nice?"

I could have crowned her. Now she'd as much as told Susan Frost how old I was. And if Susan thought I was as young as that . . . Suddenly I caught myself. Susan Frost was a perfect stranger. Why should I care what she thought of me?

My thoughts were going around in my head like torn-up paper in a high wind when Susan Frost thanked Gloria and turned to leave. Just as she went out the door, she flashed me a quick smile and tossed her head that funny way so her hair swung, and said, "See you this afternoon then, Pete," and let the screen door slam behind her.

Nobody else was in the shop just then, so Gloria looked over at me and grinned and said, "You look like a stranded grouper with your mouth hanging open, Pete. How about Miss Susan Frost of Tallahassee? Isn't she a darling?"

"Huh," I said. "I didn't notice."

Three hours later I was admitting to myself that I *had* noticed, though. I wouldn't have said it exactly like Gloria —that Susan Frost was a darling—but there *had* been something about her. I remembered with considerable surprise that I'd felt quite at ease when I was talking to her. And Susan was certainly an eyeful when it came to looks. I began to whistle as I drove the pickup north on Gulf Road —the only paved road that runs the full length of Perdido Key.

Perdido Key is about ten miles long, maybe a mile wide at its widest, and it runs roughly north and south just a rifle shot off the west coast of Florida opposite Sarta City— where I go to school—and is connected with it by a long causeway between the island and the mainland. Perdido Key's got Sarta Bay on one side of it, and the open Gulf of Mexico on the other. It's got Fiesta Village, where our fish market is, at the south end of it, and the Freebooter cottage colony at the north end. In between there isn't much of anything except flat sandy stretches of deserted landscape, some open and some wooded, between the bay and the Gulf.

I don't mean it's completely deserted. There are a good many homes ranging from mansions to shacks scattered the length of the Key along both sides of Gulf Road. I'd say the population of the Key is maybe fifteen hundred people, mostly Sarta City folks who like the isolation and quietness of the Key and commute across the causeway to work and play in Sarta City. As I say, we don't get many tourists, because Perdido is still sleepy and unspoiled. And everybody on the Key aims to keep it that way if possible.

When I realized I was whistling, I tried to figure out the reason why, because I'm not much of a whistler or singer, usually. And I finally came up with the idea that maybe I was feeling cheerful over the fact that I was going to see Susan Frost again in a few minutes when I handed over her shrimp and fish to her at the Freebooter.

One thought led to another and pretty soon I got to thinking that I'd like to date Susan Frost. After all, she was going to be here a week or so, and she probably didn't know any boys on the Key. Maybe she'd be glad to have a local guy date her a few times while she was here. And why shouldn't I be that local guy? Even if I am ugly and nervous around girls?

Then it hit me with a bang that I'd been working in the shop all day and hadn't had a shower since, and I probably smelled to high heaven of fish!

What kind of chance would I have of dating Susan Frost if I smelled like low tide in a mangrove swamp when I asked her? I worried about that until I remembered my swimming trunks under the seat of the pickup. I always carry a pair of trunks there so I can take a little dip in the bay or Gulf if I have a few minutes to spare while I'm delivering. So why shouldn't I pull off the road now and take a quick swim in the Gulf and try to wash off some of the fishiness before I saw Susan again? Before I delivered her fish? Before I asked her for a date, in other words?

It only took me a minute to make up my mind. I was about halfway to the Freebooter and on a pretty deserted stretch of road where the Key narrowed down to about half-mile width and there wasn't anything on either side of the road except woods. I'd never stopped just here before. I pulled up under a couple of cabbage palms on the right side of the road and scrabbled around under the truck seat until I found the swimming trunks. Then I put the truck keys into the pocket of my jeans where I keep my wallet and, crossing the road, I headed into the woods that lay between me and the Gulf.

The woods were pretty thick—made up mostly of live oaks, slash pine, cabbage palms, some pepper trees and Australian pines and a mild sprinkling of palmettos, sea grapes, myrtle and miscellaneous underbrush underneath the taller stuff. It wasn't hard going, though; in fact, it was open enough to let me make pretty good time.

A little way in, I could hear the Gulf surf crashing ashore ahead of me. All around me, the woods were alive with birds chirping and singing fit to kill. A mockingbird lit on a branch not three feet from my nose and began to give out with the harsh notes of a blackbird's song. As I pushed ahead toward the Gulf, I heard the subdued humming of bees coming from somewhere to my right, and a minute or so later, a strong, shrill whistle sounded from the tangle of underbrush to my left, like a cardinal's whistle, only louder. I figured it was probably the mockingbird again, showing off his copycat ways and warning me to stay out of his territory.

It took me maybe ten minutes to walk through the patch of woods before I came out on the Gulf. And I just stood there at the edge of the woods for a minute gawking at what I saw. For it was really something.

I'd come out into a beautiful natural cove with a narrow crescent beach of pure white sand as fine as powdered sugar. It stretched away to my left about two hundred yards to where a pointed tongue of land, shaped like the backward-sweeping dorsal fin of a dolphin, stuck out into the Gulf in a northerly direction to form the inlet in which I stood. To my right, the beach curved another couple of hundred yards to a point opposite the fin-shaped promontory, where the coastline of the Key returned again to its straight northerly line. The mouth of the inlet was maybe a quarter of a mile wide, and the Gulf waves came rolling in through it.

As a bathing beach, this was as nifty as anything I'd ever seen. And I hadn't even known it was here, because you'd have to come at it from the land side to see how nice it was. From the Gulf, unless you were close inshore as you sailed by the inlet mouth, you wouldn't know it existed because it was pretty well masked by that dolphin-fin tongue of land.

Anyway, it was just the thing for a quick swim to rinse away my fishy smell. I looked all around, up and down the beach, and there wasn't a living soul besides me to be seen, or a house even. Talk about privacy! The only sign of life was a quarter of a mile out in the Gulf, where a fisherman with a big straw hat was sitting in an anchored outboard with a pole over the side, drowsing in the sun while he waited for a strike. His boat was outside the inlet mouth. Maybe he lives around here, I thought, and if so, I guess he won't mind if I take a short dip in his inlet.

I went back into the woods about ten yards and stripped off my clothes in less than no time and pulled on my swimming trunks. Then I ran across the beach and through the shallow water and plunged into the surf and did a fast crawl fifty yards straight out before I turned over on my back and floated. The water felt good. I splashed, dived, rubbed my head, face, hands and arms with salt water and hoped I was killing the fish smell. I should carry a cake of soap in the truck, too, I thought to myself. Then I started toward shore, giving the beach and inlet another good look, and I just couldn't believe that they had been here all the time on the seaward side of Perdido Key and I hadn't known about them. I even had the passing thought that it might be fun to show this private cove with its beautiful beach to Susan Frost, if she was inclined to like such things.

It was getting on to four o'clock. The sun was still hot enough to dry me quickly, though. I ran up and down the beach a few times to speed up the drying process. Then I went into the woods, found my clothes, jumped into them and made tracks through the woods for Gulf Road and my truck. I took my wrist watch out of my pants pocket as I walked, and put it back on my wrist.

I came out on the road about where I'd left it—opposite my parked truck. There wasn't another car visible on the road in either direction. So I strolled across. Halfway over, I reached into my right-hand hip pocket to pull out my truck keys. And suddenly, with one foot lifted to take a step and my hand still in my pocket, I froze. I knew something was wrong.

I must have known it by instinct, I guess, because it was a second or two before I figured out that my wallet, which had been in the same pocket as my keys, was no longer there.

Well, when I got that worked out, I calmed down, because I don't carry much money in the wallet, usually, and today I knew there had been only two one-dollar bills in it. But my driver's license, my lifesaving card and some snapshots of Gloria and Pop were in the wallet, too.

I thought to myself, the stupid wallet probably fell out of my pocket when I undressed in the woods and I didn't notice it. Certainly nobody stole it . . . or they'd have stolen my wrist watch as well. And they hadn't. So there was only one thing to do. Go back through the woods and find the wallet.

I turned around, furious with myself for being so stupid, and crossed the road again to re-enter the woods. That's when I put my hand in my other hip pocket and found my wallet snuggling there safe and sound.

I froze again. Because that wasn't right, either. I knew the wallet had been in my right-hand hip pocket when I'd put the truck keys there before my swim. And now it was in the left-hand pocket. But the truck keys were still in the right one. The question that naturally occurred to me then was, how come?

There was only one answer to that. Somebody had gone through my clothes while I was swimming, searched them and put the wallet back in the wrong pocket by mistake.

In growing bewilderment, I checked the wallet's contents. The two dollars were still there. So was everything else.

THE MYSTERIOUS
PROWLER

I must have got the worst of the fish smell off because Susan didn't refuse when I asked her for a date. When she came to the door of cottage twelve at the Freebooter, I handed her the fish and shrimps and asked her for a date before I had a chance to change my mind. Much to my surprise, she said, "Wonderful! I'd love to, Pete. If Mother says it's okay. What'll we do?"

I pretended that a date with a pretty girl from Tallahassee was an everyday thing with me. I said, "Why don't we go to the movies in Sarta City? There's a good spy picture at the Crescent Theater." Then I remembered that the pickup truck was the only car we had in our family, and asked her if she'd mind riding in it. She said of course not, it sounded exciting. After that was settled, she took me in and introduced me to her mother, who was taller than Susan and wore glasses with fancy frames, but looked a lot like her with the same blue eyes and dark hair. Susan told her mother I'd asked for a date. Mrs. Frost was quite nice to me even if I was only the delivery boy with the fish for their dinner. She looked me over and chatted a minute with me;

then she smiled and said okay, if I had Susan home by midnight, at the latest. I promised. I told Susan I'd pick her up at the Freebooter at eight o'clock.

So now it was ten minutes after eight and we were driving south on Gulf Road toward Fiesta Village and the causeway to Sarta City on the mainland. Susan was dressed in some kind of a sweater and skirt deal that looked fine on her, I thought, even if I couldn't see the color too well in the truck cab. I had on my dark blue slacks and a yellow golf shirt that Gloria says I look almost human in.

A three-quarter moon was sailing over the Key. The air was as warm and balmy as summer almost, though it was only late March. In the garden of one of the houses we passed there must have been some night-blooming jasmine because we could smell it plainly, very sweet, as we drove by.

I was telling Susan about finding that inlet with the dolphin-fin headland, and what a beautiful beach it had and how deserted it had been, and so on. I told her about my swim. And when I came to the part about my wallet being in the wrong pocket, Susan said, "Why would anyone search your clothes while you were swimming, Pete?"

"It beats me," I said. "Especially since they didn't take anything."

"Could it have been a squirrel or a . . . a raccoon, maybe?"

"Not likely."

"If it was a man, you'd have seen him, wouldn't you?"

I shook my head. "I left my clothes ten yards in the

woods, and the brush was thick there. I wouldn't have seen him, even if I'd been looking for somebody, and I wasn't."

"It's pretty funny that you didn't *hear* anything, though," Susan said. She was giving my story the big treatment, as though she got a kick out of trying to solve little mysteries like this. Anyway, she seemed just as nice and natural to me tonight as she had earlier; she hadn't looked once at the scar on my cheek, or tried to get pushy or pretended to have a phony weakness for boys with big muscles or anything like that. And I hadn't once felt uneasy or awkward with her—a real switch. I began to think she was a pretty special kid. In fact, I was so busy thinking I forgot to answer her question until she asked it again. "Didn't you hear anything in the woods, Pete?"

"Nothing except the usual stuff," I said then. "Birds, and bees humming and the surf."

She said, "If somebody went through your clothes while you were swimming, he must have come from some place close by, I should think. Did you see any houses in the inlet?"

"Not a single one. The cove was empty. And I mean empty."

She kept still for a minute. I tended to my driving. Our old pickup banged and rattled, even on Gulf Road's good surface, but it didn't worry me the way it would have with some other girls I knew. Her next question was, "Where *is* this inlet you discovered, Pete?" She looked over at me and her eyes glinted in the dim light from the dashboard. "I'd love to see it. The whole thing sounds very exciting and sort of mysterious, don't you think? And I bet there *is* a house somewhere in the inlet. Where the man who searched your clothes came from."

What the heck, I played along with her. "How do you know it was a man?" I asked. "It could have been a woman just as well."

"O-oh, I never thought of that!" she said. She seemed charmed by the idea. "Where'd you say the inlet was?"

"Another mile south, I'd guess."

"Let's stop!" said Susan impulsively. "Please? It would be fun to see it."

I looked up at the moon through the windshield and pictured myself walking along that white beach in the moonlight with Susan, and I thought it might be fun at that.

I made one weak attempt to sidetrack her. "What about the movies?" I said. "That spy picture?"

"A private cove where wallets move from pocket to pocket in mysterious ways is much more interesting than a spy picture could possibly be, *I* think."

"It's just a beach," I said. "Nothing really special. What say I show it to you in daylight when we can take a swim there?" That was just a plug for another date.

"No, now," she said. "Tonight. I haven't ever had a chance to do anything as *different* as this before, Pete. I'm trying to learn to be a good painter, and I adore beach scenes and maybe the inlet you found is a place I'd like to sketch. Honestly, everything is so normal and boring in Tallahassee most of the time. You have no idea. So let's look at the cove, all right? We have to practically pass it anyway, don't we? Come on. I've seen dozens of spy movies, but not a single mysterious inlet with a tongue of land that looks like the fin of a dolphin! Please?"

I saw she was serious. So I said, "Okay."

And why not? If this is her idea of amusement, I thought, it's harmless, it's fun and it's cheap. And that's *my* idea of amusement, too. Especially the cheap. "Another quarter of a mile and we ought to be there," I said. "We'll stop and take a look if you want to."

It was full dark now, and even with the help of the moonlight, I had trouble picking out the exact spot along the featureless stretch of Gulf Road where I'd stopped that afternoon for my swim. I remembered I'd parked under two cabbage palms beside the road, but I couldn't be sure which ones, now, so I pulled up on the shoulder of the road opposite a couple of likely specimens, turned off my headlights, switched off the ignition and helped Susan down from the truck cab.

"Here we go," I said. "You aren't scared of the dark, are you?"

"Not a bit."

"That's good. Because it's going to be pretty dark in these woods until we reach the beach."

"You sure this is the right place?" She looked around.

"Near enough. Follow me close, now. I wouldn't want to lose you." I plunged in, holding branches and palmetto fronds aside for Susan to come after me.

Once into the woods, it was dark all right. Susan hung on my heels like a suckerfish on a shark's belly, and I had a sneaking suspicion she didn't feel as brave and sophisticated as she let on.

If it came to that, I didn't either. For about three minutes after we entered the woods, I thought I heard a movement in the bushes behind us.

At first I thought it was Susan making the noise. I whispered, "Whoa, Susan, stop for a minute, isn't it quiet?" and we both stood stock-still and listened. There was just the smallest bit of rustling in the underbrush back there after we'd stopped.

Susan heard it, too. She said in an unnaturally loud voice, "What are we waiting for? Where's the beach?" and urged me to move forward.

I figured that going ahead made more sense than going back. And it took less nerve, too. So I grabbed Susan's hand and started walking again, pulling her along at a good clip. She didn't say a word or even try to pull her hand away, I remembered later, but right then I was too scared to even notice that I was holding her hand. In a couple of minutes of fast walking and stumbling, we came out onto the white beach I'd seen for the first time that afternoon.

And don't ever think I wasn't glad to see it again! For as I led Susan out of the blackness of the woods into the bright moonlight of the beach, I was certain that somebody or something had followed us every step of the way from the road to the beach. And whoever it was . . . or whatever . . . made enough noise in the underbrush so even a deaf guy couldn't have missed it. It sounded as loud in the night woods as a couple of sea gulls sound outside a church window on Sunday, arguing over a fat clam.

At least, I told myself, we were out in the open now. Nobody could sneak up on us without our seeing them in the moonlight. I took a quick look at Susan and her face seemed even paler than the moonlight should have made it.

She squeezed my hand and whispered in a scared voice, "What was *that*, Pete? Behind us in the woods?"

"Probably a possum," I said. Old Pete, the nature lover! I told her the first thing that came into my head. "They mess around in the woods at night a good bit."

We walked across the beach to the water's edge—as far from the woods as I could lead Susan without getting her feet wet—and started strolling toward the dolphin-fin headland which we could see plain in the moonlight.

"Some possum!" she said. "Are you sure?"

"Well, it could have been a black bear or even a panther," I said, trying to laugh her out of her scare. She didn't know it, but an occasional black bear was still sighted on the Key, once in a long long while. "I know more about fish, actually, than I do about the night creatures of the great Florida woods."

That got a weak laugh. "You know what it sounded like to me?" she asked. We went on walking, pretending to be calm.

"What?"

"Like a *man*. A clumsy one, maybe, but a man all the same. Didn't you notice? When we stopped, he stopped."

I said, "What man?"

"The same man who searched your clothes this afternoon, probably," she answered promptly. She was a pretty logical girl.

I glanced hurriedly over my shoulder at the spot where we'd come out of the woods onto the beach. To my relief, no one was in sight. Nobody had followed us into the open, anyhow.

I said, "That's silly, Susan. What would a man follow us around at night for? And if he *was* following us, why did he quit when we came out on the beach?"

"He didn't," Susan said. "Can't you hear him?"

I could hear him all right. The sound of movement through the underbrush was keeping pace with us just inside the edge of the woods across the thirty yards of beach. I was kind of hoping she hadn't noticed, because I didn't want her to be as scared as I was. But she noticed. A sharp kid who didn't miss much, that was Susan. "So now's the time to locate a house near by where we can go and telephone for help," I said as lightly as I could, "or at least borrow a flashlight."

"If only there *were* a house! What'll we *do*, Pete? I'm scared!"

I was still holding her hand. I could feel it trembling a little bit. I had a tough time keeping mine from trembling right back at hers. "So am I," I said truthfully.

The funny thing was, that seemed to buck her up some. You know, a sort of misery-loves-company type of bucking up. Her hand stopped shaking and tightened on mine. "Shouldn't we try to get back to the road?" she asked.

"Wait." I stood still. She stood still, too, since I was holding onto her hand like grim death. Both of us strained our ears. There wasn't any doubt of it. A subdued thrashing and rustling in the underbrush inside the trees and out of our sight came clearly across the beach to us for a moment. Then it stopped, just as we had.

"He's still there," whispered Susan.

"Yep." I was trying to think what to do. I was plenty scared, more for Susan than for myself. So I said, "Here's what we do. We walk casually toward the woods, right where we just heard that noise. When he sees us coming toward him, he may run, I hope, whether he's a man or a black bear." I tried to grin at her. "When we get pretty close, I'll charge into the woods right at him. And you run back down the beach to the place where we came out of the woods. You know where that was?"

"I-I think so, yes."

"Okay. Look for our footprints in the sand if you're not sure. When you get there, cut through the woods as fast as you can the way we came, get out to the road and into the truck, pronto. Then lock yourself in until I get there. Can you do that?"

"Sure," she said. "What about you, though?"

"Don't worry, I won't try to catch him or anything. I'll just hold his attention long enough for you to get back to the truck okay. Are you ready?"

"Yes." She squeezed my hand. "Ooh, I'm really scared, Pete! I'm sorry I got us into this."

"Forget it," I said. "It's fun. Remember?"

I'd been listening hard. No more sound from the woods. So whoever was trailing us must still be in the same spot.

We walked slowly across the beach toward the edge of the woods. Ten yards from the trees, I whispered, "Now!" to Susan. She let go my hand and took off down the beach like a girl trying for the ladies' hundred-yard dash record. Her steps threw up geysers of sand that looked like white smoke in the moonlight.

I charged straight at the woods. I aimed a little to the left of where I judged those last sounds to have come from. I wanted mainly to get between the prowler and Susan, to cut him off from her. And I must have figured his location pretty accurately, scared as I was, because I hadn't covered half the distance to the woods when this loud swishing and crackling in the brush broke out a few yards to my right, and started to move away, deeper into the woods.

That figured. Whoever was in the woods watching me could see every move I made, of course. I was spotlighted on the white beach by the moonlight like an actor on the stage. As soon as he saw me start for him, he took off ahead of me.

And that was all right with me, very okay, as long as he didn't bother Susan. I was glad to let him escape, whoever he was. Especially if he was a bear or a panther. I had to admit, though, as I dashed into the dense blackness of the woods, that Susan was probably right. It was a man.

He moved through the woods like a man, anyhow. I stopped under the first trees and listened again. I could plainly mark his progress ahead of me by the thrashing of palmetto fronds, running footsteps on crackly footing and occasional thuds as he ran headlong (I guessed) into trees and creepers. And once, after one of those soft collisions, I heard what I was sure was a curse.

I felt a lot better when I realized he was trying to get away from me. The noise of his passage began to fade in front of me. I followed as fast as I could, trying to keep between him and Susan's path through the woods. Every minute or so I had to stop and listen in order to keep him located, and the first couple of times, I thought I could hear faint noises off to my left. That would be Susan, hurrying through the woods to my truck. I breathed a sigh of relief.

Now that I felt sure things were going to work out okay, I kind of let up a little in trailing the person ahead of me. I let him get farther and farther ahead, knowing that he would come out on Gulf Road a good hundred yards south of where Susan would be sitting in my locked truck.

After a while the sounds in the woods before me stopped entirely. And sure enough, a minute later I heard a starter whir, a motor catch and, after a brief roar of acceleration, the unmistakable hum of an auto being driven at high speed northward on Gulf Road.

I ran a hand across my forehead and found I was sweating. With relief, I suppose. Because there went our prowler in that departing car, and by the sound of it, he was going fast and far. Northward. Toward the bridge a mile beyond the Freebooter that connected Perdido Key with Crossbow Key. Toward Tampa and Clearwater. And a good long comfortable distance away from Susan and me . . . I hoped.

Susan. Now that the danger, if any, was past, I'd better get back to the road myself, I thought, and make sure Susan had made the truck without any trouble. So I angled off to my left through the woods, aiming at where my truck was parked. I was still too scared to want to expose myself on the open road, just in case. I didn't fool around trying to keep quiet, though. I crashed through the brush just as loudly as our mysterious follower had done trying to escape me.

My thoughts were busy, too. I was picturing Susan sitting in my locked truck cab, waiting fearfully but bravely for the hero of her adventure—me—to rejoin her, so she could tell me how calm I had been under pressure, how brilliantly I had managed her escape from unknown peril.

That just shows how wrong you can be.

Because when I came out on Gulf Road three minutes later, right opposite the two palm trees where I'd parked the truck, the truck was gone.

And so was Susan.

3 §

THE OSGOOD BROTHERS

For a second, I couldn't believe my eyes. I thought I'd mistaken the spot. They must be the wrong palm trees. Therefore the truck and Susan must be close by, either up or down the road a piece. It's hard to keep your sense of direction in the woods at night, I thought.

Then I looked northward on Gulf Road—the direction in which I'd heard the car departing minutes before. And I saw two red taillights rapidly dwindling in size as they sped away from me.

I recognized those taillights. They were shaped like shields and bigger than usual. They were the taillights of my pickup truck. "Hey!" I yelled after them without thinking. "Hey, Susan! Come back!"

They went around a curve half a mile away and winked out. I stood beside Gulf Road in the moonlight and worried.

After a bit, I thought I'd figured it out. Obviously the man who had followed us through the woods, and whom I, in turn, had followed back to the road, had had a car stashed away along Gulf Road near by. With me chasing him, he'd made it back to his car and taken off northward. So far, so good.

Now if Susan had already locked herself in my truck which was parked facing south, she had probably seen this guy dash out of the woods, jump in his car and drive past her. If so, what would she do then? Probably try to see what he looked like, I thought. Or even try to get his license number. But if his headlights blinded her so she couldn't catch a glimpse of him? With a twinge I remembered that I'd left the truck keys hanging in the ignition lock. So it was at least an even bet that Susan might have scrambled into my driver's seat, turned the truck around and started in hot pursuit of the stranger's car. In which case, I thought, there ought to be tire marks on the roadside where Susan had backed the truck to turn it.

I looked down at the sandy road shoulder at my feet, and there they were.

I felt all right then for a moment until something else occurred to me. If I'd heard the stranger's car start and drive off, why hadn't I heard Susan start the truck and follow him?

Well, that was an easy one, I told myself. I'd been making so much racket in the woods myself that I couldn't have heard a jet taking off a hundred yards away.

That's the way I worked it out. All the same, I stood there on the edge of the road as uneasy as a blue heron with a half-swallowed fish until I saw headlights coming at me from the north at a fast clip. They began to slow a little about a quarter-mile away. Then I recognized the cockeyed beam of my truck's left head lamp and stepped out in the middle of the road and waved my arms.

Susan pulled up beside me a minute later, smiling at me from the driver's seat as sweet as sugar. "Well, hello there," she said gaily. "Are you going my way?"

I grunted and she slid over and I got under the wheel.

"You had me scared," I said to her. "What was that all about?"

"While I was waiting for you in the truck, I saw somebody run out of the woods down there and zip across the road. He got into a car that was hidden under the trees, started up and turned on his lights. The next thing I knew, he drove right past me as though demons were after him."

"Not demons," I said modestly. "It was only me."

Susan laughed. "I know, Pete. I tried to see who was in the car but I couldn't. I was pretty sure of one thing, though . . . it was the man who scared us in the woods. So I just kind of subconsciously turned the truck around and followed him."

"Huh!" I muttered. "What was I supposed to think when I came back to the truck and found you'd disappeared?"

She put out a hand in an appealing gesture as I started the truck south. "I'm sorry if you worried about me," she said. "Or was it only your truck you were worried about?"

I grinned at her in spite of myself.

She went on in an excited voice, "I got close enough to the car to get the license number."

"What was it?"

"16E–714."

"Florida?"

"Yes."

"That's a rental car." I looked at Susan. "You know something? You're quite a kid." I meant it, too.

We were quiet for a minute or two. Finally I said, "I don't suppose you could tell anything about his looks when he ran across the road?"

"Only a vague impression that he was short and sort of heavyset. You know, squatty, like a wrestler."

"I sure wish I knew what he was up to," I said. "Both this afternoon with my wallet, and tonight in the woods. The whole thing gives me a feeling I don't like."

Susan said, "I think we ought to tell the police."

I considered that. "Well," I said, "it's a kind of a thin story to tell them, Susan. My wallet in the wrong pocket, and some stranger we think was following us in the woods. We were probably trespassing ourselves, when you come right down to it."

"Maybe. But what about the license number? Don't you know anybody who could find out who rented the car?"

"I know Mike Sebastien, my sister's boy friend. He's a cop."

"Then . . ."

"He thinks I'm some kind of a nut right now," I said. "You know what a guy thinks of his girl's little brother! If I tell Mike about our experience tonight, he'll think I'm out of my mind."

"Tell him anyway, why don't you? I'd like to know who was in that automobile I chased."

"How far did you chase him, by the way?"

"This side of the Freebooter. As soon as I got close enough to get his number, I turned around and came back for you. Aren't you glad?"

"I'm hysterically happy," I said, "that you remembered me at all. You still want to go to the movies?"

"Why not? It's early."

We drove on south, as full of talk as a couple of sparrows on the edge of a birdbath. As we drove across the causeway to Sarta City, Susan said, "Anyway, Pete, I *do* wish you'd tell Mr. Sebastien, that policeman, about it."

I compromised. "I'll tell Pop about it first," I said. "He was born here on the Key and knows practically everybody and every place on it, down to, and including, the black bears. If he thinks I should tell Mike, I will."

So that was the way we left it. The spy picture in Sarta City wasn't awfully good, as it turned out. I bought Susan a pizza after the show and we got back to the Freebooter by eleven-thirty. On the way, we fixed it up to go sailing together two days later, on Sunday, in one of the sailboats the Freebooter provides for its guests.

When I got home, Pop was sitting in the living room reading the newspaper as though it was morning instead of midnight. He's even bigger than I am, a couple of inches over six feet, and plenty husky. He fills up his easy chair so he makes it creak when he moves in it. His face and arms are burned brown as an old mahogany table from being out of doors so much. He's a pretty terrific guy, to tell the truth.

I sat down on our red sofa across from him, and waited until he looked up and said, "Hi, Pete."

"Hi, Pop," I said. "Any luck last night?" The old, old question everybody always asks fishermen. I hadn't seen Pop since the evening before.

"Some," he said. "We took some nice kings off Crossbow Light." He gave me a kind of quizzical look. "Gloria says you had some luck yourself today."

I let that go by. I said, "Pop, I want to ask you something. Okay?"

"Shoot," Pop said. So I told him what had happened to Susan and me in that crazy inlet that night, and about my wallet changing pockets there that afternoon. He listened to the whole thing before he said a word. He's a good listener. He put his newspaper down, and filled and lit his pipe while I talked. When I finished he said, "Whereabouts did you say this inlet was, exactly?"

"About halfway between here and the Freebooter."

Pop nodded to himself and blew out a cloud of blue smoke. "Dolphin Point," he said then. "That's what your point of land is called, the one shaped like a dolphin's dorsal. And the inlet behind it is Dolphin Inlet. Most of that strip of woods and beach in there around the cove is private property."

"Who's it belong to? I didn't see any houses."

"Couple of fellows named Osgood. Perry and Hamilton. They're brothers, unmarried, middle-aged and kind of stand-offish. Least that's their reputation since they settled down there a year or two back. Stand-offish. Most folks don't even know they're in there, and those who do keep away from them because they're so grouchy and crusty, usually. They like their privacy, I guess. So I reckon you *were* trespassing when you went in there for a swim, Pete. And when you took Susan in there tonight, too." He took his pipe out of his mouth and gave me a grin. "Gloria says this Susan is a real dish," he said. "How about it, Pete?"

I pretended my ankle was itching and scratched it. I shrugged. "Look, Pop," I said, "where do the Osgoods *live*?"

"In a little beat-up beach cottage around the other side of Dolphin Point. They bought it from an old fisherman named Jude Skanzy along with the land around it about a year ago, I think. Got it for peanuts, too, the way I heard it."

"The other side of the point?" I said. "You mean you can't see their house from the inlet side?"

"Nope. It's pretty well hidden by a stand of trees. You can make it out from the Gulf, but only barely. It's so weathered and needs paint so bad it kind of blends into the landscape. You got to look hard to make it out at all."

"Do you think it was one of those Osgood brothers, then, who moved my wallet this afternoon, Pop? And followed Susan and me tonight?"

Pop shrugged. "Sounds like them. They don't like anybody butting into their inlet, I know that. I suppose they were curious about who you were this afternoon and took a look at your driver's license, maybe, while you were swimming, to find out."

"Why would they follow Susan and me tonight?"

"Same reason. Wanted to see what you were up to in their bailiwick." Pop grinned at me again. "Those two shellbacks don't recognize romance when they see it, of course. Wouldn't understand a boy and a girl taking a simple walk in the moonlight together. You got to remember that."

I shook my head. "It still seems queer to me, Pop. What do those birds *do* out there?"

"Fish a lot, I guess," Pop answered. "They keep a couple of boats in a short blind canal on the inner curve of Dolphin Point, I know that. I've seen them fishing in the Gulf occasionally from an outboard, and doing some scuba diving from a bigger boat."

I remembered the fisherman I'd seen in the mouth of Dolphin Inlet. "I guess I saw one of them, then. The other Osgood brother must have searched my clothes."

Pop knocked the dottle out of his pipe. "Pete, I don't know exactly what the Osgoods' line is, but they must be interested in studying Gulf currents, or underwater geology, or marine biology or something to do with marine research, anyway, because it seems to me I've heard that once in a while they bring in specimens of various kinds to the marine laboratory down on Halfmoon Key. Anyway, they're harmless, that's for sure. Before they bought the Dolphin Inlet property they used to drift around Florida a lot, although they were born right here on the Key. They even took a trip to Europe not long back, the way I remember it. Their father was a handyman and plumber and left them a few bucks when he died. They blew most of it on that European trip, I guess—on that and the Dolphin Inlet property and their boats."

"Then what do the old buzzards live on now, Pop?"

"Search me. They seem to get along all right." He fixed

me with a severe look. "And what's more, Pete, I don't like your calling the Osgood brothers 'old buzzards.' Buzzards, maybe, but not old. Is that clear?"

"You said they were middle-aged."

"That isn't old." Pop was forceful. "I'm middle-aged my-self, so I know. And Perry Osgood is just about the same age as me."

"He is?"

"Yep. He was in my class at high school, matter of fact."

"Oh. So that's how you know so much about them?"

"Sure. It's over twenty years since we were in school." Pop stood up and his easy chair creaked. He went to our bookcase beside the closed door to Gloria's room. Gloria was sound asleep inside, so Pop kept his voice low when he said, "Perry's picture is here in my high school year-book." He pulled his tattered yearbook out of the book-case and turned the pages for a minute. Then he came over and held the book open for me to see. "That's him," Pop said. "The 'old buzzard' who spoiled your walk with Susan in the moonlight."

The picture showed a lean-faced, serious-looking kid with a sharp chin and big ears that seemed to stick out pretty far because of his narrow head. He had a lot of curly hair but hardly any eyebrows. Perry Osgood hadn't been any prize-winner for looks, I could see that, but who was I to talk?

Pop said, "Perry was tall and skinny when he was young, and he's still that way." He flicked a finger against Perry's picture. "Doesn't look much like a guy to be scared of, does he? Even in the woods at night."

"I wasn't exactly scared, Pop. I was just kind of worried about Susan."

"Sure." Pop kidded me with a straight face. "That's only natural."

"Well," I said, "maybe I was a little scared." I frowned. "If it was one of those Osgood brothers trailing us in the woods, how come he turned tail and ran when I charged him? It was *his* property."

Pop said, "With the moonlight, whoever was spying on you could see you plain as day. All of a sudden you come roaring across the beach at him. You're a big husky kid, Pete. You look fighting mad. With the result that *you* scared him more than he scared you." Pop nodded. "He's afraid you'll catch him and clobber him, even if he is on his own property. The Osgoods never were what you'd call real brave, Pete."

I said, "What about the car he took off in?"

Pop's shoulders went up in a shrug. "What about it? It was a rental car, you said. The Osgoods don't own a car themselves, far as I know. And there's a hundred reasons why they might rent one temporarily. You scared him so bad he wanted to get away from you fast, that's all. So he used the car that was right there handy."

"Would it be parked on Gulf Road?"

"Sure. That's the closest you can get to the Osgood shack with a car."

I stood up. "Well, thanks, Pop. Susan thought I ought to tell the police—or Mike Sebastien, anyway—about it. But if it was one of those Osgoods who followed us, I guess I won't. Would you?"

Pop put his yearbook back in the bookcase. "Forget it," he advised. "You accidentally ran into one of the Osgood boys tonight, that's all. And he tried to check up on a couple of snoopers in his private cove and got chased for his pains."

"Okay." I started for my own room. Then, remembering Susan's description of the man who had run across the road, I asked one last question. "What's Perry Osgood's brother look like, Pop? Hamilton Osgood, is that his name?"

"Everybody called him Ham," Pop said, "when he was a kid. He was ten years younger than Perry and me. And built real close to the ground. Six inches shorter than Perry, the way I remember him. But I haven't laid eyes on him for years."

"That was Hamilton spying on us tonight, then," I said. "Good night, Pop. It's been a big day."

Pop picked up his newspaper. "Good night, son."

I shut my door and got undressed. I felt tired and fresh, let down and excited, sleepy and wide awake, all at the same time. I was yawning my head off but all of a sudden I kind of hated to waste time sleeping when there were such interesting things to think about as Dolphin Inlet and the Osgood brothers. And Susan.

You know what I mean?

4 ❧

SUSAN MAKES
A DISCOVERY

The next day was Saturday. I knew I'd be as busy as a minnow dodging sea gulls because next to Friday, Saturday is our biggest day at the fish market, and I always have plenty of cleaning and filleting to do for customers, besides a lot of deliveries to make.

I was sort of looking forward to it, though, because it would bring me one day nearer to Sunday when I had another date with Susan Frost.

Isn't that something? Here I was, just putting in time, you might say, until I could see Susan again, and I hadn't even met the girl twenty-four hours ago! The all-new Pete Hobbs, I thought to myself as I worked over a fat pompano for Mrs. Hendricks. The sophisticate, the man-of-the-world, the cool, poised dater of pretty girls from Tallahassee. I began to whistle under my breath.

Gloria heard me. She looked over at me between waiting on customers and gave me the big smile that says, "Aha, Pete! I *told* you she was a doll!"

About ten-thirty I heard an outboard motor coughing its way up our channel from the bay. This channel is a short curving one from Sarta Bay that dead-ends right beside our fish market in a little landlocked pool where Pop ties up his boat. There's always a mess of empty baskets and fish crates and scales and nets and miscellaneous fishing gear kicking around there, but it's handy for Pop because the channel gives our boat access to the bay . . . and, through Sunset Pass, to the Gulf itself.

Anyway, I heard this outboard coming up our channel. It died out with a last gasp at our dock. And a minute later, somebody came into the market, letting the screen door slam behind him. It didn't surprise me much that a customer should come up our channel by boat, because that happened fairly often. What shook me up was the customer himself.

I took a casual look at him when he came in and when I realized he was a stranger I'd never seen before, I turned back to the cleaning table where I was working on a black grouper for Mrs. Casey. A half second later, I did a quick double-take and came near cutting off my thumb with the fish knife. For all of a sudden it hit me that I'd never seen this customer before in the flesh, maybe, but I *had* seen a picture of him. Only last night, in fact. In Pop's high school yearbook.

There couldn't be two guys with that long sharp chin. And the sticking-out ears. And the crop of curly grayish hair on a narrow skull. And with that tall skinny build besides, and no eyebrows. He was older but he was the same guy, all right.

Perry Osgood.

There were three customers ahead of him in the line

waiting for Gloria to take their orders. I put down my knife and stood and stared at him for a minute before I could get myself to operating again. What was *he* doing here? He'd never bought fish from us before. I couldn't help remembering Pop's suggestion that one of the Osgoods had taken a look at my driver's license while I was swimming in the inlet. If so, then Perry Osgood knew who I was and where I lived. Was that why he was here? To find out about me, look me over, talk to me?

"Mrs. Casey's waiting," Gloria called to me. I came out of my trance and finished filleting the grouper. Gloria wrapped it up. I started on a mackerel.

A shadow fell over my cleaning table. I looked up. And there he was. Standing right where Susan had stood yesterday admiring my "economy of motion," whatever she meant by that. Some art term, maybe? She'd said she was a painter.

Perry Osgood said in a raspy voice, "Are you Peter Hobbs?"

I went on scraping scales off the mackerel. "Yes, sir," I said. "My sister will wait on you over there at the counter. I just clean the fish."

He tried to be friendly. "You're pretty good at it, too."

"Thanks." Then, like an idiot, I said the same thing I'd said to Susan yesterday. "It's all in the knife."

Grinning, "That's what I always say, too," Osgood commented. He was quiet a second. I went on working. "Reason I asked you, are you Rusty Hobbs's boy?"

"Yes, sir. That's Pop."

"Oh." A shade of warmth, interest, relief in his voice? I wasn't sure. "I used to know him, years ago."

"That so?" I wasn't going to help him.

"Yep. So now he owns a fish market! You doing any good with it?"

"What do you mean?"

"Making any money?"

"Pop's main business is fishing," I said shortly. "This market is just a sideline."

"Still," Osgood said, strangely persistent, "I guess a lot of people come to buy from you, don't they?"

"Quite a few, yes, sir." What did he think? After all, it's a fish market.

"People from the Key?"

"Mostly."

"Winter visitors, too, I imagine?"

"Some. Not many tourists on the Key. Do you live on Perdido?" I asked him innocently. "I don't remember seeing you before."

"Yep. Up north a way. Dolphin Inlet." Out of the corner of my eye, I could see he was giving me a sharp glance when he said that.

I pretended I'd never heard of the place, which I hadn't, till last night. "Oh," I said, acting uninterested. Then I thought, what the heck, if he's so curious, I'll give him a little of his own medicine. I said, "You haven't ever been in to buy fish from us before, have you?"

"Nope." Perry Osgood shrugged his narrow shoulders under the sun-faded blue work shirt he was wearing. "Ain't got a car. And this is pretty far by boat just for fish. We catch our own fish mostly, anyway." I noticed he said "we."

I remembered how this guy's brother had scared Susan and me—half to death. I said, "Then what brings you in *this* time all of a sudden?"

He hesitated before he answered that one. He flicked an eye to our display case to see what we had for sale. Then he explained in a hale-and-hearty kind of way, "Couldn't resist trying your snapper, I guess, son. Heard about it for years. People say it's almost like a different fish, as though it was caught in some hole in the Gulf that nobody else knows about. Fellow mentioned it just the other day, so as I happened to have an errand down this way . . ."

He broke off as Gloria finished waiting on Mrs. Kreiling and called to him, "Can I help you now?"

He nodded and said, "Two of those small red snappers in the case, please, miss. Whole. Just the way they are."

Gloria reached into the case for the snappers. "Don't you want Pete to clean them?"

"I'll handle that myself," Osgood said. He didn't move away from my cleaning table. "Just wrap 'em up, please."

While Gloria was wrapping his fish, I said, "It's nice to hear that our snapper is popular. Who did you say told you about it?"

He paused. Then he said slowly, "Oh, some fellow, probably one of the winter visitors, not a local man, I kind of forget who." Osgood put up a knobby-knuckled hand and rasped the day-old beard on his sharp chin. "Now what *was* that guy's name?" He snapped his fingers. "Got it!"

he said. "It was a fellow named Roscoe Chapin. Do you know him?"

I looked up into his eyes. They had the cold intentness of 12-gauge shotgun muzzles. He was watching me like a hawk. Why? To see if that name registered with me?

I shook my head. "Roscoe Chapin? No, sir. I never heard of him, far as I can remember. Did you, Gloria?" After all, she works alone in the shop when I'm in school and knows our customers far better than I do. She said she'd never heard of Roscoe Chapin, either.

The intentness faded out of Osgood's eyes. He must have thought we were telling the truth. Which we were. At least I was. The name Roscoe Chapin didn't ring any bells with me.

Osgood took his package of fish from Gloria and paid her. I thought he looked relieved.

"Nice to meet you, Pete," he said to me as he left. "Tell your father I said hello after all these years. And thanks very much, miss," he said to Gloria.

"Who'll I tell Pop was saying hello?" I asked, just to be sure.

"Perry Osgood. He probably won't remember me. From Sarta City High."

"I'll tell him, Mr. Osgood," I said. He went out, and it wasn't long until we heard his outboard start up and go racketing down our channel to the bay.

Twenty minutes after Osgood left, a car pulled up in front of the shop and another customer came in to join the three or four who were already waiting their turns with Gloria. I was on the telephone at the time, taking an order for smoked mullet from Mrs. Canaday, and I had my back to the counter so I didn't see right away who it was.

As I hung up the receiver, Gloria said in a certain kind of voice, "Pete," and I swung around and there was Susan Frost.

I felt my Adam's apple give a twitch or two. "Hi, Susan," I said, keeping it cool and natural, as though I wasn't tickled half to death to see her.

Susan came over by the tubs and said in a low voice, "Can you come outside for a minute?"

I stropped my knife on the whetstone. "Sure," I answered. "Soon as we get these customers taken care of. Maybe five minutes?" I looked at her closely then, and I could see that she was really excited about something, for her eyes were shining like calm water in a low sun. I wondered what it was, and I was half tempted to walk outside with her right then and find out, making the other customers wait a few minutes, but I couldn't do that, of course.

Susan nodded and touched my wrist with the tip of her finger and turned toward the door. That finger touch was like being touched by a mild electric current. "I'll be outside," she said in a voice so soft that nobody else in the market could hear her. "In the car."

I guess I never cleaned and filleted fish quicker than the ones I did in the next few minutes. When the last customer went out with her package, there was a lull, so I whipped off my apron and said to Gloria, "I'm going outside for a minute, sis. To talk to Susan. I'll come right back in if another customer shows up. Okay?"

Gloria put a hand up to her hair in the grand manner she likes to put on sometimes. "What! Quitting right smack in the middle of our busiest morning?" She was indignant. Then she grinned impishly, "Get on out there, dope, before she decides to find herself another fellow!"

Gloria's pretty crude sometimes about stuff like that.

I followed her advice, though. I took the whole flight of steps in front of the fish market at one jump. Susan was sitting behind the wheel of a gray Chevy thirty feet away. I went over and opened the door and climbed in beside her.

"I couldn't wait to tell you about it, Pete!" she said before I even got the car door shut.

"What?" I said.

"Something I found out this morning."

"You're killing me. Give."

"It's really not very much, but I felt a sort of personal interest."

I pointed one finger at her like a gun and said, "In what? I've only got a few minutes, Susan. What happened?"

She told it straight, then. "After breakfast this morning, I was walking down to the beach at the Freebooter . . . you know, on that path that goes by the swimming pool and all the cottages . . . and I was noticing the states the cars in the cottage carports came from. And when I came to this one cottage, number eighteen, it had a dark-blue sedan in the carport. And when I looked at *its* license plate to see what state it was from, what do you think, Pete?"

"What?"

"It was a Florida plate. And this is the exciting part—the number was 16E–714!"

I felt a thrill go through me. I told myself that license number didn't mean a thing, but I felt this stab of excitement, anyway.

When I didn't say anything, Susan shook my sleeve. "How about that?" she cried. "Don't you recognize that number? It's the one I got last night when I chased that car! It belongs to the man who scared us in the woods!" She was awfully pleased with her detective work, I could tell that. "Why don't you say something? Is anything wrong?"

"No," I said, "except that the car doesn't mean anything, Susan. I told Pop what happened to us last night, the way I promised I would, and he explained everything very simply, even the car."

"Well!" Susan said, and sank back against the car cushion like a deflated baloon.

I gave her a sketchy account of what Pop had told me about the Osgood brothers. "Perry Osgood, the older brother," I finished, "was in the fish market himself not half an hour ago. For the first time. Only thing I can figure is, he came in to check up on me, see who it was who took a swim in his precious inlet yesterday, without his permission. He gave me a phony story about some guy we never heard of, named Roscoe Chapin, recommending our red snapper to him. But that was just a gag, I'm pretty sure, just an excuse for coming in. When he found out I was Rusty Hobbs's son, he decided not to give me a hard time over trespassing in his inlet, I suppose. Probably felt ashamed of himself, too, for sneaking that look in my wallet since I turned out to be Rusty Hobbs's kid."

"But how about last night?" Susan asked, her eyes big.

"The other brother. Hamilton Osgood. So there goes our big mystery, Susan."

Susan made a face. "Isn't that the way!" she said. "My absolutely first mystery, darn it! And now your father's taken all the fun out of it!" Her mock-rueful expression didn't quite come off. She was enjoying some private joke of her own, I suspected.

"Who needs mystery?" I said. "Tomorrow we're going sailing. *That*'s fun."

"I know. I guess I'm silly. I did enjoy the excitement while it lasted, though, didn't you?"

I tried to be honest. "Well," I answered, "maybe a little. But what I enjoyed more than the excitement was being with you when it happened."

Can you beat it? To come out with a corny crack like that?

Susan gave a whistle. "Hey!" she cried. "What nice things these fishermen say!"

I switched in a hurry. "So what Hamilton Osgood is doing at the Freebooter with his rented car parked by cottage eighteen I don't know," I said hastily.

She gave me a slanting glance. "Huh-uh," she said.

"What's that mean?" I asked her.

"It isn't Hamilton Osgood, Pete."

"At the Freebooter? With the car?"

"It can't be," Susan said, "unless the records are wrong."

"What records?"

"At the Freebooter." She was teasing me. "Or else the car must have been rented again to somebody else since last night, Pete."

I started to open the door to get out, for Mrs. Loring was going up the steps to the fish market and I'd be needed inside. "What are you talking about?" I said to Susan.

"Listen," she said, "when I saw that license number this morning, I went into the Freebooter's office and asked the girl at the desk who was occupying cottage eighteen. She looked it up for me in the card file of guests. Same license number. But it wasn't anybody named Osgood."

If Susan wanted to keep me in her car for another few seconds with that news, she succeeded. I stared at her. "It's got to be," I finally said. "Why, the car was heading right for the Freebooter when you chased it last night. And how could it be rented to somebody else so fast? Pop said . . ." My voice trailed off as I saw where my questions were leading me. I looked at Susan. "It *wasn't* Hamilton Osgood who trailed us last night, then?"

Susan said brightly, "Evidently not."

"Then who was it? Who's occupying cottage eighteen at the Freebooter?"

She let me in on her private joke. "It's a fellow named Roscoe Chapin," she said.

5 ❧

A VISIT TO
DOLPHIN INLET

The next day was just right for sailing. The Gulf was flat
and lazy and breathing deep, as we say, but with enough
liveliness in the water to make sailing fun, and a four-knot
breeze from the southeast. The sun was bright and hot.

I drove up to the Freebooter in the pickup after lunch.
Susan and I took one of the little Sailfish sailboats they
supply their guests with, and sailed south along the coast
of Perdido Key about half a mile out.

I handled the boat, and Susan sat there with her legs
in the well and her hair tied in a ponytail with a blue ribbon,
looking slightly gorgeous and telling me about Roscoe
Chapin.

"I caught a glimpse of him this morning, Pete. He's
dark and short. And quite sinister-looking, really. Even in
broad daylight."

I was feeling good. I didn't want to talk seriously about
anything just then, least of all Roscoe Chapin. I said, "We
can't be *sure* it was Roscoe Chapin in the woods, Susan.
After all, if you got just one digit of that license number
wrong the other night, it could have been almost anybody."

"I didn't get any digits wrong!" Susan said. "I was close enough to see the number very plainly. Besides, Roscoe Chapin *looks* like the wrestler type you chased out of the woods—squatty and low-slung. Isn't that suspicious?"

I nodded at her. "I guess so. Suspicious enough so I've thought about it a lot. And all I can come up with is that if it was Chapin who followed us through the woods, he has to have some connection with the Osgoods, because Perry Osgood mentioned his name to me. You see what I mean?"

"Of course. Mother always told me I had a natural talent for intrigue. So why was Chapin following us?"

"I don't know. Unless he ran into us by accident and was curious."

"But what was *he* doing in the woods? Do you think he could have been spying on the Osgoods?"

"Search me." I tacked in toward shore. "We ought to be about opposite the mouth of Dolphin Inlet here," I said.

I knew what Susan would do. And I was right. She half stood up in the well and said, "Wouldn't it be fun to sail in close enough to see their house? The Osgoods'?"

"Watch the boom," I said. "Sure, why not? That's why I mentioned it."

A minute later she said, "I can make out Dolphin Point now, I think. Isn't that what you said it was called?"

"Yep." I squinted under the boom at the shoreline. "There's the house."

"Where?"

"Under those slash pines toward the base of the fin. Sort of a nothing gray color. See it? It's real little."

"I see it!" We were getting closer. "Pete, it looks a hundred years old."

"Probably is, too." We were rapidly nearing the mouth of the inlet now, and I was about to lay the Sailfish over on the other tack and beat to seaward again when I got this crazy idea. It was absolutely none of our business, but I thought it might be interesting for Susan to meet the Osgood brothers and see their house for herself. Not to mention how curious *I* was!

So without even checking with Susan, I took a quick look at the set of the tide and the wind, and let our sail down with a bang. At the same time I reached forward, grabbed our centerboard and pulled it up free.

"What's happening?" Susan asked in a startled voice.

"How'd you like to visit the Osgoods?"

"Now? Right now?"

"Sure."

"Oh, dear!" Susan didn't sound too enthusiastic. "Are you going to tell them somebody followed us through their woods Friday night?"

I shook my head. "Not a word. All that would do is tell them I was trespassing *again* on their property . . . twice the same day. And had the nerve to bring a girl along the second time!"

She laughed. "Are you serious about going in?"

"If you're game," I answered.

With our sail down and our centerboard up, our little boat bobbed like a cork on the Gulf and, directed by the tiller, drifted quickly toward shore near the Osgoods' house, as I had figured it would. The Gulf was too calm for us to be in any danger of capsizing. Susan didn't know that, however. She said in a small voice, "Watch out, Pete! I think we're going to bump the shore! And it's terribly rocky!"

"Relax," I said. "Here's the idea, Susan. Our sail has jammed a little and I want to see if I can fix it. That's what we'll tell the Osgoods. Maybe we'll get a chance to look around Dolphin Inlet while we're at it."

Susan said, "Look, there are two men in front of the cottage."

"Reception committee," I said. There were a lot of big boulders along the water's edge, as Susan had pointed out, so I didn't look up from my steering until we had drifted safely ashore and scraped our keel gently in the shallow water not a stone's throw from the Osgood shack of pecky cypress. Even then, I pretended to fool with our sail rings until Susan gave a forced laugh and said, "Oh, I'm sorry if this is your private beach, but something's wrong with our boat, and we thought we'd better . . ."

She floundered and I came to the rescue. "It seems to be all right now, Susan," I said. Then, putting surprise into it, I said, "Hi, Mr. Osgood! Is this your house?" Perry Osgood and his brother were standing a few yards away, watching us. "I'm Pete Hobbs from Hobbs's Fish Market, do you remember me? I talked to you yesterday when you bought some snappers from us. And this is Susan Frost from Tallahassee. She's staying at the Freebooter."

"Hello, Pete," Perry Osgood said pleasantly enough. He didn't introduce his brother who was standing beside him, a balding, hook-nosed man with thick lips and the tense squint of the nearsighted. "Run into trouble with your boat, eh?" He peered closely at our Sailfish. "Nothing serious, I hope."

I threw a fast look at their house which was set on the fin-shaped ridge, a few feet above sea level. "Nothing to worry about," I answered him. "The lines seemed to catch there for a minute, wouldn't run free." I tried a smile on Hamilton Osgood. He smiled back noncommittally. Then his eyes switched to Susan. And I couldn't blame him for that.

Susan was saying enthusiastically, "Oh, what a darling cottage, Mr. Osgood! I'm a beginning painter, and I'd *love* to paint your house! It's got marvelous character."

With that, she leaped ashore as lightly as a fluff of goose down and started toward the Osgoods' shack with a long limber stride that was something to see, dressed as she was in bathing suit and lifebelt, with a huge beach towel wrapped around her shoulders and arms to keep off the sun.

I looked apologetically at the Osgood brothers and said, "Susan's nuts about Florida beach scenes, sir. Do you mind?"

Ham Osgood still didn't say anything. Perry said, "Of course not, Pete." He sounded hearty. "She's welcome to look around as much as she wants." He turned to his brother. "I went to school with this kid's father. Remember Rusty Hobbs?"

Only then did Hamilton Osgood nod and relax a little from his neutral stance, as though Perry had said, "These kids are okay."

"Thanks, Mr. Osgood," I said. "We can only stay a minute." I tied the sailboat's painter to a handy rock and started after Susan, splashing through the shallow water. Perry and Ham Osgood followed along, giving the impression that they rather enjoyed entertaining teenagers on Sunday afternoon.

Susan was standing in front of their shack by this time, admiring its weathered beauty out loud. It was about as beautiful as an old shredded wheat carton, but artists can get away with calling anything beautiful, I guess. And Susan knew it.

As the four of us drifted around the house on a sandy footpath that began at the front door and disappeared around the house corner, Susan was going on about the artistic attractions of Dolphin Point and the Osgood cottage at a great rate. She got really enthusiastic about a small rustic lean-to that was built onto the back of the house. It was a weather-beaten old enclosure that at one time must have served the original owner of the house, Jude Skanzy the fisherman, as a catch-all for nets, oars, lobster pots and other fishing gear. Its sagging door, held by a rusted latch, gave on the path that came around the house from the front door. The rear of the house faced into the inlet but was concealed from it by a stand of slash pines and a few live oaks.

We walked through this screen of trees, and there below us was Dolphin Inlet, a glittering sheet of busy water that flashed in the sunlight like fish scales. I said, "Did you ever see a niftier beach, Susan?" pointing to it.

Susan had seen that beach for herself only two nights ago in the moonlight, but she acted now as though it were all new to her.

Neither of the Osgood brothers said a word all the time we were admiring their house and their view. They seemed pleased that we liked their home, however.

Finally I saw what I was looking for—the gleam of still water in the heavy growth of palmetto and palms below the Osgood house on the inner curve of the headland to our left. The path from the house ended down there, apparently. I pretended surprise. "Is that a canal, Mr. Osgood? Is that where you keep your boat?"

"Boats," he corrected me. "We got two of them."

I started for the canal through the brush and trees, along the path that led from the back of the house. "Gosh, I'm interested in boats," I said. "I want to be a commercial fisherman like Pop. Do you mind if I take a look, Mr. Osgood?"

"Help yourself," Perry Osgood said genially from behind me. "Our specimen boat ought to interest you."

"Specimen boat?"

"Yep. The boat we use for diving and gathering marine specimens. And getting bottom samples," Perry said easily. "We spend most of our time in or under the water out here, you know that?"

"You do?"

"Yep. We're underwater hobbyists, you might say. Only amateurs, of course. But it beats playing golf or fishing off the bridges for passing the time. Occasionally we even find something of interest to the marine laboratories down on Halfmoon Key."

Perry led Susan and me to the far end of the blind canal where two boats were tied up. His brother trailed along behind us, still silent, although his eyes had kindled a bit, it seemed to me, when Perry talked about their underwater activities.

The skiff with the outboard motor that Perry had used to come to our fish market was tied up to a long rickety wooden dock that edged the canal. Just behind it lay the specimen boat.

It *was* interesting, I'll say that for it. It must have been a converted Navy launch or some similar craft, for it was fully thirty feet long and wide in the beam, with a lot of flat deck space fore and aft of the deckhouse. A movable boarding ladder of aluminum that could be hung over the side lay on the deck amidships below the low rail. The rest of the deck space was pretty well cluttered up with diving gear of various kinds; compressed air tanks, face masks, neoprene diving suits, air hoses, water pumps, haul-up baskets on long hand lines and a couple of spearguns with their missiles, half covered by a tarp. There was a wide-mouthed pipe arrangement, too, like an old-fashioned stovepipe. I'd never seen anything like it.

"What's this thing?" I asked Perry Osgood, pointing to it. Perry had followed me aboard. "The thing that looks like a vacuum cleaner?"

He smiled. "That's our own idea," he said with what seemed real pride. "Rigged it up ourselves. It's a dredge we built to help us suck up samples of Gulf bottom for analysis."

"What's the use of analyzing Gulf bottom?" I asked.

"Ever hear of striking oil in the Gulf, offshore? You can

tell a lot from bottom samples, Pete. And you never know —we might get lucky."

"How's the thing work?"

For the first time, the other Osgood brother, Hamilton, opened his mouth. "Works with a water pump and a hose," he explained, "to create suction through the pipe and to the surface."

"Oh," I said, "I see." His voice was a surprise. It was as soft and well modulated as Mr. Neuman's, my English teacher at Sarta City High. Judging from his harsh, hawk-faced appearance, I'd expected Ham Osgood's voice to be rough and tough.

I turned around to say something to Susan, and found she'd walked with Perry Osgood to the other side of the deckhouse to admire the view from the short canal into Dolphin Inlet. They were talking a mile a minute. Nobody could resist Susan's naturally appealing ways for long. I knew that from personal experience.

I said to Ham Osgood, "I guess it was you I saw fishing the other day when I trespassed on your property by mistake and took a swim in the inlet?"

"Friday?" Ham said in his smooth voice. "Was that you? About four o'clock? Yes, I was fishing in the outboard, out in the Gulf. I saw you swimming and running on the beach." He didn't acknowledge my indirect apology for trespassing, nor invite me to come back for another swim sometime, but he went on pleasantly, "Perry and I both are fond of fish. So we fish a great deal. For food as well as specimens."

"What do you catch, mostly?" I asked idly.

"Mullet. They're quite plentiful usually."

"I didn't notice your net," I said. "I thought you were using a pole."

"I was. I can usually catch enough mullet for the two of us with hook and line," he explained.

"What do you use for bait? Live shrimp?"

"Yes." He made a leisurely move toward the dock. I followed him off the boat. Susan and Perry Osgood were ahead of us.

When we caught up with them, I said, "I sure envy you some of that diving gear! I love to dive myself."

"Well, it's mostly secondhand," Perry said frankly, "but it works all right."

We went back to our sailboat on the Gulf side of Dolphin Point. Susan waded a few feet out and climbed aboard. I untied the painter and followed. As I shoved off, Susan was fluting, "Your house and this point are so darling! Thank you so much for letting us see them, Mr. Osgood." I raised our sail, grabbed the tiller and, when the water was deep enough, I dropped the centerboard in the slot. "May I come back, please, and paint them sometime?" Susan begged.

"Just a beat-up old shack, miss," Perry answered, "seems a silly thing to paint. But if you want to, come ahead. We're usually here." Did he hesitate a fraction of a second before issuing that invitation? I wasn't sure.

Our sail took the breeze and we quickly widened the distance between us and the Osgoods, who stood gazing after us from the boulder-strewn shore in front of their cottage. I raised one hand to them, they returned the salute, then I gave my attention to sailing. The breeze had freshened a little while we were visiting the Osgoods.

Susan sat very quietly for a few minutes with the beach towel draped around her like a blanket. She looked like a pretty squaw. Finally I said to her, "Boy, talk about a performance! Are you as good an artist as you are an actress?"

"Better," she said, "but I wasn't too bad, was I? And we did get a look at their place." Then, on a faint note of regret she said, "But they didn't seem exactly *sinister* to me, Pete. I thought they were nice."

After a short silence, I said, "Perry Osgood is probably a marine expert as advertised, Susan. But his brother Hamilton is not."

"Oh? Why not?"

"Because no marine expert would think of going fishing for mullet with hook and line and live bait. And that's what Ham Osgood told me he was doing when I saw him fishing Friday afternoon."

"I don't get it."

"Mullet is a vegetarian fish. You catch mullet in nets . . . and only in nets. Once in a long long time a real patient fisherman may be able to catch a mullet on a little bitty hook hidden in a streamer of seaweed, or with a snatch pole off a bridge when the tide's right. But not with a regular rig and live bait!"

"You're joking!" she said.

"No, I'm not. Pop's a fisherman, don't forget. And I know a little bit about stuff like that, too." I patted her shoulder through her towel to soften the impact of what

I was going to tell her next. "What's more, Susan, I'll make you a bet right this minute that Hamilton Osgood *isn't* Hamilton Osgood!"

Her mouth opened in amazement. "He isn't?"

"I don't think so. Pop remembers Hamilton Osgood as ten years younger than his brother Perry, and six inches shorter. How tall was that guy today?"

"Almost as tall as Perry. Within an inch or two."

"Right. And how old would you say? Older than Perry or younger? At a rough guess?"

"Older," Susan said in a shocked voice. "He's bald and that makes a difference, I suppose, but I'd say older. Quite a bit older."

"That's what I thought, too." I hauled around onto the starboard tack. We ducked the boom. "So how about *that?*"

Susan recovered fast. "Couldn't your father be wrong?" she asked. "Anyway, after seeing them and talking to them, you can't tell me those two shy men could be doing anything mysterious or . . . or . . . illegal, Pete! They said I could come back and paint their cottage whenever I wanted to, don't forget. And they showed us around like perfect gentlemen."

"Yeah," I admitted. "There's still something funny about them, though. And that wasn't Hamilton Osgood, I'll bet you. There's nothing wrong with Pop's memory."

"Then who was it?" Susan asked.

"Search me." I was thoroughly confused.

Susan's eyes sparkled with excitement. "Let's call him Mr. X," she said. "That sounds kind of mysterious and sinister, doesn't it?"

6 ✆

WHO IS MR. X?

That evening, before Pop took his boat out on the Gulf, I had a chance to talk to him for a few minutes alone. Gloria was riding around with Mike Sebastien in his patrol car, having what she called a "traveling date." Mike was on duty every other Sunday night and had to stay within reach of his shortwave to answer any calls that might come in from headquarters.

I brought Pop up to date on everything that had been happening: Perry Osgood's visit to our market at the recommendation (so he said) of a man named Roscoe Chapin; Susan's tracing of the rental car to cottage eighteen at the Freebooter which was occupied, apparently, by this same Roscoe Chapin; our afternoon call on the Osgood brothers at Dolphin Inlet by sailboat.

I finished, "So we're pretty sure it wasn't Hamilton Osgood who followed us through the woods the other night, Pop. Susan and I think it was the fellow named Roscoe Chapin."

Pop stopped sucking on his pipe and said, "I never heard of anybody named Roscoe Chapin, Pete."

"Neither did Gloria," I said. "And neither did I."

"So Perry Osgood is getting a little befuddled, I wouldn't wonder," said Pop, blowing smoke. "After all, he *is* middle-aged, you know." He chuckled. "Can't remember names any more, probably. Like me. Or remembers the wrong ones. What's so serious about that?"

"Nothing," I said, "except it seems kind of hard to put a finger on Hamilton Osgood, Pop. You thought that's who was following us the other night in the woods. And it wasn't. And *we* thought, Susan and I, that it was Hamilton Osgood out at Dolphin Inlet today with his brother Perry . . . only it wasn't."

Pop lifted one eyebrow at me. That meant he was surprised. "You said there were two of them at the inlet," he protested.

"There were two men there, all right," I said. "And one of them was Perry Osgood. But the other man, who didn't say much and acted as though he was pretending to be Hamilton Osgood, wasn't Hamilton Osgood. Or Roscoe Chapin, either. At least, I'm pretty sure he wasn't."

"Then who was he?" Pop said, reasonably enough.

"We don't know. This guy was almost as tall as Perry Osgood, and you said Hamilton was short and chunky. He was also older than Perry, at least he looked older. And you said Ham Osgood was younger."

"I also told you that middle-aged men get befuddled, Pete." Pop grinned at me. "Maybe I was remembering Ham Osgood all wrong." He was needling me a little, but I didn't pay any attention.

"And the funniest thing was about the mullet fishing," I said. I told Pop about that.

He listened quietly, serious now. When I finished, he tapped out his pipe and looked at his wrist watch. It was almost time for him to leave. We could hear his crew arriving in their rattly old car outside. He said, "Did Perry Osgood actually introduce this other man to you and Susan as Hamilton Osgood? Or did he call him 'Ham' while you were there?"

"No-o," I was forced to admit after thinking back.

"Then forget it," Pop said briskly. He stood up and stretched. "He wasn't Ham Osgood and they weren't pretending he was. He was probably just another friend of the Osgoods, like that fellow Chapin. Or some scientist helping them with their marine research, maybe. You and Susan just happened to go calling when Hamilton Osgood was away from the house on an errand. Or taking his Sunday afternoon bath indoors!"

I wagged my head back and forth. I was feeling stubborn. "That guy's no scientist, Pop," I said. "You've got to admit he doesn't know much about marine life if he says he fishes for mullet with live shrimp!"

"What if he's an oil geologist? Or an engineer, Pete? He might not know beans about mullet fishing then."

"Why wouldn't he say so?"

Pop paused in the doorway. "Lot of fellows don't like to admit they don't know much about fishing," Pop said. "Especially civilized types." He grinned at me. "Anyway, I'll tell you one thing for sure, Pete. If I was your age and had a date with a pretty girl on a Sunday afternoon and a Sailfish supplied free to take her sailing in, I wouldn't waste much time worrying about an ugly old boy like Osgood!"

With these parting words of wisdom, Pop went out and joined his waiting crew. A minute later, I heard his motor begin to rumble quietly. Then the sound went away down the channel toward the bay, slow and dignified.

For the first time in a long while, I didn't sleep very well that night. I kept dreaming that I pulled in one of Pop's mullet nets and there was Hamilton Osgood with a white featureless face like the off side of an egg, caught in the net among the fish. The only thing was, he had long brown hair like Susan's, and kept tossing it back over his shoulder with a sidewise motion of his head.

Mondays are a little bit slow so I didn't really have enough work to keep me busy the next morning. I buried a dozen pint buckets of oysters in the chipped ice in our display case (we had to import them from Apalachicola because our own oyster beds were contaminated) and I arranged our mullet, pompano, snapper, trout and kings in the case to look as appetizing as it's possible for dead fish with their mouths open to look, and then settled down to ducking Gloria's questions about Susan.

About eleven, Mrs. Terrill came in and bought some fish. She's the wife of Dr. Terrill, the director of the Marine Lab down on Halfmoon Key south of us. She began to gossip with Gloria about her daughter's forthcoming wedding to a chemist from up North, so after I'd filleted her fish I went outside for a break, leaving them talking. I found Dr. Terrill smoking a cigar in his car, listening to some rock-and-roll on the car radio.

We'd known the Terrills ever since we were kids, so I went over and said hello to him. "Mrs. Terrill's telling Gloria about Nancy's wedding," I said. "She'll be out in a minute."

"Hi, Pete," Dr. Terrill said. "Women are something when they've got a wedding to talk about, aren't they?"

"Seem to be," I agreed. "Gloria's been talking for eleven months steady now about her own, and she and Mike Sebastien haven't even fixed on a date yet."

Dr. Terrill laughed. He reached over and switched off his car radio. "Why you kids think that racket is *music* I'll never understand," he said.

"Sure it's music," I said. "It's got a real good beat to it." Dr. Terrill was always kidding his own children and anybody else's he met about rock-and-roll, "I'll admit that a lot of singing groups really ham it up these days, but . . . " and that reminded me suddenly of Ham Osgood. I said, "I met the Osgood brothers from Dolphin Inlet a few days ago, Dr. Terrill. And Pop says they're interested in marine research of some kind. Don't they bring specimens to you at the lab every once in a while?"

"Yes, occasionally."

"What kind?"

"Well, last winter for example, they brought me a small mako shark they caught in Dolphin Inlet. Its stomach contained a can of screen paint that had been bought from a paint dealer in Key West."

"Paint?"

"Sure. They thought it might help me in my studies about the geographical distribution and peregrinations of sharks."

"I haven't heard about paint in a shark before," I said, interested in spite of myself. "That's a funny one."

"Not as funny as some other things found in sharks' bellies," Dr. Terrill said. He was kind of an authority on sharks. "Like the waterproof packet of documents that a sea captain suspected of piracy had thrown overboard to prevent its confiscation. Two years later, the documents were found in a shark's stomach and were used to convict the pirate and hang him."

Pop had told me about that one. I switched back to the Osgoods. "Do the Osgoods really know very much about marine science?" I asked, kind of offhand.

Dr. Terrill gave me a puzzled look. "They're amateurs, of course," he said. "But enthusiastic ones. And they *have* helped me in the past. Why?"

"Oh, I'm just curious about them. Hamilton Osgood talked about mullet as if he didn't know a mullet from a mangrove snapper."

"That's funny," Dr. Terrill said, "because they brought me jellyfish specimens with enlarged red granules in them during our last red tide here, as well as other plankton to study in connection with it. If they're interested in helping me analyze a phenomenon like the red tide, they ought to know a mullet from a mangrove snapper, I should think."

"Yeah," I said. I knew enough about the red tide to hate it and fear it, like everybody else on the Keys and coastal areas of the Gulf. When we get a red tide, the water turns a kind of pinkish-red color from an overabundance, near the surface, of plankton with red granules in their bodies. Pretty soon the plankton (some of the organisms are microscopic bacteria and some are as big as jellyfish) begin to die and decompose so fast they deplete the amount of oxygen in the water. That's what Dr. Terrill says. Then an awful-smelling scum forms on the water and millions of fish die from lack of oxygen. The dead fish are washed up on the beach and lie there and rot with an unbelievable stench unless they're buried or carted away. During a red tide, a vapor rises off the water and irritates your eyes and nose and makes you cough a lot, just as though you had a bad cold. Even if you live a couple of miles away from the beach. Nobody knows much to do about red tides, but believe me, they're murder while they last! Sometimes it's just for a few hours. And sometimes it goes on for a couple of weeks until the water gets mixed around enough so the amount of plankton is normal again. You can see that everybody would be scared stiff of a red tide. Especially fishermen like Pop. I was plenty scared of red tides myself, ever since I had to help bury tons of dead fish that were washed up on Fiesta Village beach during a red tide when I was thirteen.

Mrs. Terrill came out of the market with her package of fish in her hand. Before she got to the car, I said hurriedly, "Do *both* the Osgood brothers bring you specimens, Dr. Terrill? Or only Perry?"

He hesitated for a second, thinking back. Then he said, "Only Perry, I guess. He's the tall skinny one with no eyebrows, isn't he? But he talks about his brother Hamilton as though they were both research buffs. I can't remember meeting Hamilton himself."

Just then, Mrs. Terrill came up. I opened the car door

for her to climb in beside her husband. She thanked me and said, "Remember, now, Pete, I know how boys hate weddings, but we're expecting you to come with Gloria and your father to Nancy's next month!"

"I'll be there," I promised, lifting my right hand solemnly. "I swear."

We all laughed, and Dr. Terrill drove off. I watched them go, and through the rear window of their car, I could see Dr. Terrill lean forward to switch on the car radio again— probably for some more of that rock-and-roll he pretended he didn't like.

I went back inside the market and killed a little time going over our list of standing orders, although I knew them all by heart. When Gloria took a ten-minute break at half-past eleven and went into our house behind the market to powder her nose and fix up a snack for our lunch, I looked up the telephone number of the Freebooter in the book and called Susan's cottage.

She answered the phone herself.

"Hi," I said, "you know who this is?"

"Of course. Who could mistake that gravelly baritone? Aren't you working?"

"Sure. But it's slow this morning. And I wanted to tell you that I talked to Pop last night about those Osgood brothers. He still thinks I'm a nut to worry about them." That wasn't the only reason I'd called her, of course, but it seemed like a pretty good excuse.

"Did your father think our Mr. X *was* Hamilton Osgood?" Susan asked.

"No. He thinks it was probably some friend. A casual

visitor. He says Hamilton Osgood was either away from home yesterday or taking a bath when we were there."

Over the phone, her laugh sounded as pretty as musical chimes.

"What's more," I said, "I asked the director of the Marine Lab if he'd ever met Hamilton when the Osgoods brought specimens into the lab. I was hoping we'd get another description of Hamilton to settle the thing. But Dr. Terrill only knows Perry."

"We saw them this morning," Susan said.

"Who? The Osgoods?"

"Yes. At least, Perry Osgood and Mr. X."

"Where?"

"Over in Sarta City, just pulling into the marina in their outboard."

"They don't have a car, so I guess they must have been going shopping in the boat."

"That's what I thought."

I began to get an idea. "How long ago was that, Susan?" I asked her.

"Oh, half an hour ago. We were starting across the causeway to Perdido Key on our way home."

"Half an hour," I said. "They can't cross the bay, get through Sunset Pass and up the coast of Perdido to Dolphin Inlet in less than an hour in that outboard of theirs. Even if they started back right after you saw them."

"What are you thinking of?"

"Well, I'm just curious enough about who Mr. X is, and about Dolphin Inlet, to feel like going out there while they're safely in Sarta City and looking around a little bit."

"Pete! You wouldn't! It's none of our business, after all. And even if it's been fun rigging up a little mystery for ourselves, I don't think . . . "

"You want to paint their house and the point, don't you?"

"Yes, but . . . "

"And maybe you could make a couple of sketches or something today when they're away, couldn't you? They *said* you'd be welcome to paint the place, remember."

She weakened. "You're supposed to be working, Pete." Her tone was severe, but I could tell she was as interested as I was now in going to Dolphin Inlet.

"I know. But I told you it's awful slow today. And maybe I can get Gloria to handle things for an hour here. If I can, will you meet me out there?"

Susan said something to her mother, evidently about lunch, because when she came back on the phone, she said, "Mother says it's okay if we don't stay long. We'll have lunch afterward."

"Me, too," I said. "So unless I call you back right away, I'll meet you on Gulf Road where we left the truck the other night. By those cabbage palms. Okay?"

"How soon?"

"Fifteen minutes."

"I'll bring a sketch pad."

"And I'll bring a mask and some flippers. Maybe I can get a quick look *under* Dolphin Inlet, too!"

"See you in fifteen minutes," Susan said.

7 ℘

UNDERWATER
ENCOUNTER

Susan was waiting for me in her car under the cabbage palms on Gulf Road when I arrived opposite the inlet. She got out of her car as I parked my pickup beside it and held up a big sketch pad in one hand and a couple of charcoal pencils in the other.

"Hi!" she greeted me. "I still think this is a crazy idea, Pete, but I'm ready for action if you are." She had on the same shorts and blouse she'd worn the day I met her.

"It could be a crazy idea, all right," I agreed, climbing down. "Probably is." I had changed into swim trunks at home. Now I pretended to be busy getting my flippers and mask out of the truck. "But this crazy idea is giving me an excuse to see you in the middle of a working day, so why knock it?"

I turned around and looked at her then, surprised at my own nerve. She blushed a little bit and smiled. "Okay, fisherman," she said, "cut out the soft talk and let's get moving before Mr. X and Mr. Osgood get back from Sarta City."

We went quickly through the woods together toward

the Dolphin Inlet beach. Susan glanced around her at the thick underbrush and the spooky-looking Spanish moss that was hanging from some of the trees and her shoulders shook. "I'll never forget how scared I was the other night," she said, "when that man followed us here in the dark!"

I nodded. "I was plenty scared myself. If I ever get a chance, I'd like to scare Mr. Roscoe Chapin as bad as he scared us."

"*If* it was Roscoe Chapin," Susan said. "We're not sure of that, even."

"Sure enough for me to hate the guy, anyway!"

We came out on the beach and headed for Dolphin Point, whose curving scattering of trees hid the Osgood shack from our view. There wasn't a sign of anybody in the inlet or on the water today. We reconnoitered around the point. The blank windows of the Osgood house stared back at us like empty eye sockets. I watched for five minutes without noting any movement in or about the shack.

Susan was already sketching away on her pad, and from what I could see, she seemed to have a real flair for drawing, because the Osgood cottage took shape with astonishing speed in a series of bold, unhesitating pencil strokes that caught the dilapidated and weather-beaten quality of the place to the life. If she can paint as well as she can draw, I thought to myself, she's a pretty talented kid! Just then, Susan looked up from her pad and said in a matter-of-fact tone, "You'd better start looking around, Pete, if you want to get out of here before they get home."

I left her sketching and went down the path that led to the blind canal where the Osgoods kept their boats. The specimen boat creaked against the rotting dock. After a minute's survey to make sure it was unoccupied, I went aboard for another quick look at it.

I didn't see anything I hadn't seen before. Through the windows of the deckhouse I could see nothing but a massive clutter of the same sort of miscellaneous gear that littered the deck. Ropes, pull-up buckets and baskets, frayed air hoses, a rusting compressor. Obviously the Osgoods didn't spend many nights aboard their specimen boat, for there weren't any sleeping accommodations. I decided the specimen boat had at one stage in its career been a naval launch, meant to ferry sailors from ship to shore. I took note of the fact that there were two neoprene diving suits on board, two complete sets of scuba gear. And I admired again the odd vacuum-cleaner device which Perry Osgood had told me could suck up samples of Gulf bottom.

When I rejoined Susan, she was standing under the slash pines beside the house and still sketching. As I came up, she said, "I think this is the angle for my painting, Pete. It composes better from here than the front view from the Gulf. And I can get in that picturesque little lean-to at the back."

"Great," I said truthfully, looking over her shoulder at the sketch. "Great economy of motion." Even a fisherman could tell that her black-and-white sketch would make an attractive painting in color. She made a swipe at me for kidding her about the economy of motion stuff.

I reported to her on my search of the specimen boat. "There are definitely two divers working from that boat," I said, "because there are two sets of everything."

"Is that supposed to mean something significant?"

I shrugged. "I don't know. It might mean either that Hamilton Osgood *does* dive with his brother Perry, or that Mr. X is a diver himself. But all three of them can't dive at the same time, because there are only two suits."

Susan laughed. "Maybe the third one doesn't dive. I should think somebody has to be running that big boat while the others dive."

See what I mean? A pretty sharp girl. I said, "Yeah. And anyway, there may be a third set of diving gear in the house. Or maybe they sometimes dive from the outboard."

"They use the outboard mostly for fishing and shopping, I should think," Susan said. "Mr. X was fishing in it when you came swimming, wasn't he?"

I started. "That's right. He was. Fishing for mullet with live bait, he told me with a straight face. Maybe he wasn't fishing, after all. Just pretended to be."

"Why would he do that?"

"Search me. To keep me from suspecting that he was doing something else, maybe."

"Like what?"

"Like diving."

"Diving? From that little outboard boat?"

"Sure. Why not? It's perfectly possible. You anchor the outboard in shallow water . . . " I stopped, struck by a sudden recollection.

"What's the matter?" Susan asked. She had stopped sketching and was watching me.

"I just remembered that whistle I heard as I came through the woods for my swim."

"What's that got to do with anything?"

"Maybe," I said slowly, "it could have been a warning."

"You mean somebody was whistling at Mr. X out in the boat?"

I nodded. "It's possible. It might explain why Mr. X gave me all that jazz about mullet fishing. He's not really a fisherman but he wants me to think so, see?"

"No," said Susan simply. "I don't."

"Well," I said, "suppose Perry Osgood or Hamilton Osgood, whichever, happened to be in the woods between here and Gulf Road and saw me—or heard me—coming into their precious private inlet? And suppose they didn't want anybody to know that Mr. X was diving out there on the water? So Perry or Hamilton whistled loud enough for Mr. X to hear. A prearranged danger signal. And Mr. X, who happens to be in the boat at the time and not underwater, puts a fishing pole over the side, claps on a straw hat and fakes the fishing scene. And when I called him on it yesterday, he dreamed up that fairy tale about mullet fishing?"

"But why? Why would they go through all that rigmarole?"

"I told you. To keep me from suspecting that Mr. X was actually diving out there and not fishing."

Susan shook her head at me. "You're the absolute limit, Pete!" she said. "What an imagination! Just answer me one little question: why would they care in the slightest whether anybody knew they were diving or not? After all, your father and Dr. Terrill both told you they bring specimens to the laboratory. And *they* told you yesterday themselves that they dive all the time, and even look for oil. And they showed us their diving boat yesterday. They're making no secret of the fact that they dive. So what's all the excitement about?"

I had to admit that was a pretty good question. And the answer to it, I realized all of a sudden, was why I'd had this sneaking desire to take a look *under* Dolphin Inlet—why I'd had the crazy impulse to bring a mask and flippers with me today.

I said, "Look, Susan. Maybe the Osgoods and Mr. X don't care who knows they're diving at Dolphin Inlet. What they want to keep secret is *where!*"

"Oh!" she said. I could see the idea hitting her. She was quick. "So if they've discovered a promising spot for an oil well or something, they don't want anybody else to know where it is? Is that what you mean?"

"Sure." I looked at my watch.

"Should we be leaving?" Susan asked.

"I'm sure we've still got a good half hour before they can make it home," I said. "They had to spend some time in Sarta City. I think I'll swim out there where Mr. X was fishing, and take a look at the bottom."

Susan's eyes went to the expanse of Dolphin Inlet. She turned back to me with a frown and put one hand on my arm. "The water's pretty rough, Pete," she suggested, "even inside the inlet. Do you think you'd better?"

"Sure," I said, "no problem." The weather station had forecast a thirty-mile wind by evening and there were already whitecaps on the Gulf, but I didn't think there would be any risk in just swimming out beyond the inlet mouth and taking a peek below.

"Don't stay long," Susan said. "I really wish you wouldn't try it."

I grinned at her. I felt good enough to swim eight miles in a hurricane, it was so nice to have her worrying about me. I said, "A few little waves won't bother me, Susan. I'll be fifteen minutes at the most."

"What if Mr. X and Mr. Osgood come back and find me here alone?"

"Remember the rough water will slow them down, too. They'll have to crawl in that little outboard. There's plenty of time."

"All right." She closed up her sketch pad and walked down to the beach with me. "Hurry up, Pete. And *you* remember, please, that only Mr. X and Perry Osgood are in Sarta City in the outboard. So where's Hamilton Osgood? Taking another bath? *He* might show up any minute."

"I don't think so," I said. "No matter what Pop says."

I waded out from the beach and took off for the mouth of Dolphin Inlet in an easy crawl, turning to lift one hand at Susan, who stood on the beach and watched me until I got well started, then walked up the rise to the Osgood house again.

I had often swum in rougher seas; it was no trick at all to reach the inlet mouth. Outside, though, in the open Gulf, the water was rougher and although the swimming was easy enough, the waves made it hard for me to locate, even approximately, the place where Mr. X had anchored in the outboard. It was tough to get any kind of a fix from landmarks because the waves kept hiding them from me. And a pretty good rip tide was going there beyond the inlet mouth. It tossed me around enough so I couldn't get properly oriented.

I wasn't about to give up on that account, though. When I got to a spot about where I thought Mr. X's outboard had been anchored, I gulped in a couple of big breaths of air that was now growing cool, and dived. With my flippers scissoring behind me and my eyes looking ahead through the glass of my mask, I swam strongly for the bottom of the Gulf, hoping it wasn't too far below the surface here.

It wasn't. I touched hard ridges of gray sand with my hands at what I figured might be maybe fifteen feet. I peered around me with as much curiosity as a cat in a fish market, looking for something—anything—that might represent the object of Mr. X's diving efforts.

I hardly need to say that I didn't see anything. Not only because there wasn't anything there to see except sand bottom with a scattering of shell, rocks and waving sea grasses, but because the wind, tide and surging surf off the inlet mouth had combined to stir up sand, seaweed, algae and everything underwater into such a swirling turmoil that visibility was reduced to about elbow length. I should have realized what I'd find before I swam out here. I'd been too interested and curious, I guess (or too anxious to show off before Susan) to think very clearly about it.

Anyway, it was all too plain that I'd wasted my time. I wasn't in the right spot in the first place, I was fairly certain of that. In the second place, as I said, the visibility was practically zero. And what was I expecting to find, anyhow? My blood started to thud in my ears, warning me that I was about out of wind and ought to surface soon. If I'd only been halfway smart and brought scuba gear, I was thinking, so I could stay down for more than a minute at a time . . .

I'd got this far in my thoughts when an incredible thing happened. It happened so fast, and so unexpectedly, that I was hardly aware of it until it was all over. Yet I've never known anything that actually lasted such a short time to seem so endless. The last part of it, at least. And if you think that sounds confused, it is. Because I was about the most confused kid in Florida at that particular second.

I was holding onto a rock on the bottom, anchoring myself against the surge of the water and trying to make up my mind to surface and give up this crazy business, when out of the corner of my mask I caught a glimpse through the cloudy water of what looked like another swimmer.

I thought I was dreaming. And then I saw it again. It was real. It was alive. It was a man.

Whoever it was, he seemed to be brighter than I was, because I imagined I could make out some cylindrical shapes on his back which could only be compressed air cylinders. The bubbles rising in front of his head confirmed it. He was swimming along the bottom of the Gulf at a fair rate of speed, wagging flippered feet behind him and traveling, as near as I could make out through the murk, on a course that would pass my own position maybe five feet off to the right.

I was so surprised at seeing this crazy sight fifteen feet down in the Gulf, all wavy and indistinct because of the violent water disturbance, that I forgot for a split second my urgent need for air. I just hung onto my rock, staring like a fool at the shadowy shape. The underwater silence pressed on my eardrums.

My first thought, naturally enough, was that Perry Osgood and Mr. X had somehow returned from Sarta City earlier than I expected, and that this was one of them, making up a little diving time after shopping all morning. Or—the second idea that popped into my head—maybe it was Hamilton Osgood who was swimming there beside me, and the reason we'd never seen hide nor hair of him was because he spent all his time underwater! Which was a silly thing to think, you must admit.

It shows you how wild I was. My heart started to thump against my ribs like a diesel chugging in an echo chamber. My air was all used up. All I could do was to go up to the surface, get some fresh air in my lungs and swim back to Susan as quick as I could.

I let go of my rock. I squatted, flexing my legs for the big push upward.

And then, at that exact second, the other swimmer caught sight of me! I could tell by the way he checked his forward movement, by the thick stream of bubbles he gave off, by the head-on view I suddenly got of his face mask. Then I noticed something else about the strange swimmer that made the Gulf water feel awfully cold all at once.

The guy had a speargun in one fist.

I could see it as he came to a dead stop and grabbed hold of the same rock I'd been hanging onto only a few seconds ago. He was less than four feet away. So what, I thought, trying not to panic. Plenty of scuba divers carry spears. For fishing . . . for fun. So why worry about this fellow?

It was a good try, but I couldn't find much comfort in it. Because as I strained my eyes to see more clearly through the cloudy water, I suddenly knew with terrified certainty that I *did* have something to worry about.

Slowly, slowly—it seemed to take forever—I saw the mysterious swimmer's speargun come around until its barbed, razor-sharp point was aiming directly at me. Then, to my utter horror, I saw a thick, sausagelike finger curl with incredible slowness around the trigger of the gun and deliberately jerk it back.

The missile flashed toward me. If it hit me, I knew it would spit me as neatly and cleanly as a five-pound barracuda. And with the same fatal results.

8

THE MESSAGE IN
THE BURNER BASKET

I acted by instinct, I guess, when I saw that fat finger begin to curl around the speargun trigger. Even at that, I was almost too late. I gave a hard push against the Gulf bottom with my feet—such a tremendous heave, in fact, that it's a wonder I didn't burst up through the water and take flight into the sky like a Polaris missile.

As I shot upward, I felt a gentle touch along the side of my right thigh and knew with sickening relief that the fish spear had missed me. Or almost. I say almost, because when I lowered my eyes for a second I saw that there was a small cloud of pinkish water trailing behind my kicking right leg. And I knew the color of the water was caused by blood, my blood. Bad aim, poor visibility or just plain good luck had prevented the spear from hitting me dead center. And I do mean dead! I was more than glad to settle for the loss of a little blood.

The same glance downward that showed me the blood showed me something else that sent a big wave of relief through me and helped quiet my nerves. The guy down there who had taken a shot at me was in a little bit of trouble himself. He was still hanging onto that rock on the bottom, but a surging swell coming out of the inlet had swept his feet from under him and turned him upside down, so that his flippers were pointing up toward the surface while his hands clung to the rock that anchored him. He would be as helpless for a few minutes, I knew, as though he'd been tied in that awkward position with ropes. For I'd had the same thing happen to me a few times when I was diving. A surge hits you and knocks you topsy-turvy. You grab hold of a rock or something to stay put so the next surge won't sweep you back. Your heels are over your head and every surge twists you, and you swear the whole world is swinging around you like crazy. You get completely disoriented. You get dizzy. You can even get violently seasick sometimes. And that's a pretty bad thing to be when your mouth is plugged up with a breathing tube!

Anyway, my unknown attacker had his hands full down there for a few minutes. He couldn't follow me right away, even if he wanted to take another crack at me. I felt great about that.

Then I thought, maybe he didn't really take a crack at me. Maybe he wasn't trying to murder me. Maybe he only wanted to scare me a little. If that's what he wanted, brother, it sure worked! I was practically as scared as I was mad. Or maybe, my thoughts kept circling around, he took me for somebody else because of the poor visibility? And he was trying to kill *him* and not me?

Just then, I broke the surface of the Gulf. I pulled in some deep breaths of wonderful air, noticed with surprise how beautiful everything looked up there, and started to swim for the beach inside Dolphin Inlet as though my life depended on it. And maybe it did, for all I knew, because my leg was still bleeding and I didn't need Dr. Terrill's knowledge of sharks' habits to know that blood in the water could easily attract them.

So I made the beach in record time. Don Schollander couldn't have covered the distance any faster. I waded out on the sand, and there was Susan waiting for me, looking almost as worried as I felt.

Her eyes fell to the shallow groove the spear had cut along the side of my thigh and she saw the blood running down my leg. "What happened to you, Pete?" she said. Her voice sounded strange, but she didn't turn pale or faint or anything like that, the way a lot of kids will do at the sight of blood. She twitched her handkerchief—or whatever girls call that three-cornered scarf they wear—off her head and wadded it up in her hand and slapped it on the cut in my leg. "Hold that on there," she told me, "until we get to the cars. I've got a first aid kit in mine."

I put down my hand and held the wadded cloth in place and started to follow her down the beach toward the place where we could cut through the woods to Gulf Road.

"What *did* happen?" she repeated, holding onto my arm as if I was so weak I needed her help to walk.

"No time to tell you now, Susan," I panted. I was still blowing from my swim. And from fear, too, I guess. "Let's move a little faster, shall we? I'm fine . . . but I want to get out of here quick!"

"Okay." She began to run beside me and it reminded me of the other time when she had run down this same beach, frightened by something or somebody in Dolphin Inlet. It was getting to be a habit, it seemed.

We zipped through the woods. I was limping a little as we ran, because I had to hold the cloth on my cut, but it didn't slow us down much. We came out on Gulf Road right across from the cars, dashed over and climbed into the front seat of hers. She yanked open the glove compartment and fished out a little Red Cross first aid kit and opened it up on her lap.

I felt real relaxed, now, and a little bit heroic again, to tell the truth. It was kind of nice to have Susan fussing over me. Now I could examine my leg, I could see the cut wasn't anything at all—three-quarters of an inch long and not deep enough to need a stitch, even. It was bleeding some still, but a large-size Band-Aid soon put a stop to that.

She put away the first aid kit. "Now," she said to me, leaning back behind the wheel of the car, "come on, Pete, what happened?"

I told her. Every detail as nearly as I could remember it. She listened with her lips apart a little and her eyes as big as ashtrays. When I ended my story, she was just as mad at that murderous scuba diver as I was.

"He could have killed you!" she said indignantly. "What kind of a fool is that to have running around loose?"

I had to laugh. "He's probably thinking the same thing about me. Especially if he thought I was a shark."

Susan said with disdain, "Shark! You don't look enough like a shark for him to make a mistake like that. Pete, who *was* it, do you think?"

Knowing the answer before I asked, I said, "Perry Osgood or Mr. X?"

She shook her head. "No, Pete. They didn't come home."

"Hamilton Osgood, maybe?" I told her about my silly thought under the inlet, that Ham Osgood stayed underwater all the time like a fish. She said she hadn't seen anybody in the inlet while I was swimming out there.

"Okay," I said. "So it could have been anybody. There are a million scuba divers come to Florida every year on vacation, and a lot of them like to dive off the Keys here on the west coast."

Susan said, "You don't really believe it was a tourist, do you?"

"Could be. They panic easy."

Susan turned her head and frowned out the window beside her. Then she turned back after a minute and put two fingers into the pocket of her blouse. She pulled out a little piece of paper, folded once. When she opened it out, I could see it was black and charred along three edges.

"What's that?" I said.

"Part of a letter. I found it while you were swimming."

"At the Osgoods'?"

She nodded. "There's a place at the back of their house where they burn their rubbish and stuff. In a big wire basket. This must have blown out of the burner basket. It's partly burned, see? I found it when I walked around to the back of the cottage to sketch it from that side."

I took it out of her hand and read the few lines of writing you could still make out on the partially burned paper. Here's what they said:

. . . delighted you are working so hard on our project. I am kept informed of your progress and will expect my full share at the end. Don't try to cross again. It isn't safe. Remember the cured ham.

R.C.

Susan said, "What do you think about that, Pete?"

"It's Greek to me. Seems like part of a letter, all right, but I haven't any idea what it means. It's private correspondence, Susan, and we probably shouldn't . . ."

Susan said, "The initials, Pete!"

"Yeah. R.C. For a signature."

She bit her lip. "Well?"

"Roscoe Chapin?"

"Of course! Who else could it be?"

I laughed again. "A million people, Susan. There must be at least that many with the initials R.C."

"You don't *really* think that letter was signed by Ruth Corwin or Robinson Crusoe or Rannie Clunk, do you?"

I grinned at her sarcasm. "Well, I admit Roscoe Chapin's name seems to keep popping up all over the place around here recently, ever since we got interested in Dolphin Inlet," I said.

"I'm glad you admit it." She gave her head a shake. "And when it comes down to it, it could have been Roscoe Chapin who tried to kill you just now, couldn't it?"

I hesitated. I'd been thinking the same thing. "He's one possibility, sure. *If* the guy actually tried to kill me. Roscoe Chapin could be doing a little scuba diving off Dolphin Inlet as easy as anybody else, I suppose."

"See?" Susan cried triumphantly. "You think so, too!"

"And so?" I could see she was getting ready to give me some kind of an argument.

"I think you ought to tell the police about it, that's all!" she said earnestly. "I thought so in the first place, and I think so even more now that you've been wounded by that man under the water. And now that I've found this letter signed R.C.!"

I sighed. "You're probably right, Susan," I said. "And right now, I'm mad enough at that character to report him to the F.B.I., the C.I.A. *and* the Supreme Court! So I'll tell Mike about him."

"All right. Will you promise to tell him all about this business? *All* about it? Promise?"

"Sure," I said. "I have the feeling I'd be nuts not to, as a matter of fact. First thing tomorrow."

"Why not now?"

"Today's Mike's day off. And besides, I have to get back to work."

She smiled. "That's right of course. Well, good-by, then, and don't forget."

"I won't." I got out of her car and went to our pickup truck and got in. I said, "Thanks for the efficient first aid, Susan."

"It was a pleasure." She backed her car to turn it.

"It was a pleasure for me, too," I said. She straightened away and headed north, waving.

I waved back. Then I turned the truck and headed for home.

The wind was freshening, backing around to the north-east. The first time the Gulf came into view from the road, I could see the waves were getting up fast. Heavy surf was pounding in along the Key. The air was chilly. The sun had disappeared under a gray overcast. It looked as though we were in for a pretty decent spring storm.

I wondered whether Perry Osgood and Mr. X in their little outboard would be able to make it through the growing waves of the Gulf to Dolphin Inlet.

9 ✌

MIKE SEBASTIEN
LENDS A HAND

The storm blew itself out during the night. When I went to see Mike Sebastien at police headquarters in Fiesta Village next morning, the sunshine we're so proud of in our state was back again. The Gulf was still kicking up rough, but the wind was gone.

Gloria, of course, was full of curiosity when I asked her to handle the market chores alone for an hour or so, and started to kid me about Susan taking up all my working time. She was more curious than ever when I told her I wasn't going to see Susan, I was going to see a certain Mike Sebastien, a member of Perdido Key's police force.

She said, "Why don't you telephone him, Pete?" which was a sneaky way of trying to learn what it was all about. She figured to listen to my end of the conversation on the fish market phone. I broke down and told her the whole thing then, because I knew Mike would tell her anyway. So she shooed me out of the market about quarter to ten when things were quiet for a while.

Mike is a black-haired, black-eyed, good-looking fellow who stands six-three in his socks and causes most of the girls on the Key to practically faint when he looks at them. In his uniform, driving the Key's only patrol car, with the police emblem on the side and the red bubble on top, he's pretty handsome, I guess. He's half-Spanish and half-Seminole Indian and a great guy, actually, even if I do pretend to Gloria that I think he's a jerk just to tease her sometimes.

Anyway, Mike was alone in the one-room headquarters, which is only big enough to hold two desks face to face—one for Mike and one for Sergeant Carroll, his superior—along with a couple of uncomfortable straight chairs, a gun rack on the wall, a water cooler in one corner and, in a converted closet outside the door of the office, a telephone switchboard and police transmitter in charge of Edna Jennings, a sharp old lady who used to teach kindergarten in Sarta City. Edna Jennings knows me, because I was in her kindergarten class, so she sent me right in to see Mike.

"Hi, Pete," he said to me, "how's Gloria?" All I do is remind him of my sister. I sat down in one of the straight chairs.

"She's okay," I answered him. "Mike, have you got a minute? I'd like to tell you about a funny thing that happened to me yesterday . . ."

His black eyes glinted at me. "You mean police business?"

"I guess so, Mike."

"Shoot," said Mike. "What happened to you that was funny?"

"A guy tried to kill me with a speargun under Dolphin Inlet," I said.

He stared at me. "That's funny, all right. Hilarious. You kidding?"

I told him the whole thing as fast as I could talk. Mike lit a brown paper cigarette and listened to me without a word.

When I finished, I wasn't a bit surprised to have Mike wag his head at me and say, "Pete, I think you're maybe making a big thing out of a lot of little unrelated incidents that really don't mean much by themselves."

"Maybe," I said, "but I'd hate to get killed by one of those unrelated little incidents, Mike."

He grinned. "Who wouldn't? But take it from the top, Pete. If your wallet was searched while you swam at Dolphin Inlet, you can't complain. You were trespassing. If somebody followed you and Susan in the woods, what can we do? Maybe they had as much right there as you did. Or maybe they thought *you* were following them! The rental car being used by a guy named Roscoe Chapin doesn't prove a thing about Roscoe Chapin himself. He rents a car, he can use it any way he pleases. This Mr. X could be Hamilton Osgood or the Governor of Alaska, it's none of our business until he breaks the law. The R.C. initials on this note"—Mike tapped the charred paper I'd given him—"could be anybody, as you pointed out yourself. And anyway, what can we do on the basis of a piece of partially destroyed private correspondence that you kids stole . . . yeah, stole . . . out of Osgood's burner basket?"

He was going to brush it all aside as meaning nothing, I could see that plain as day. I said, "Mike, you may be right about all those incidents. But it's a little more serious to the police when somebody tries to kill somebody, isn't it? I wasn't trespassing then. I was out in the open Gulf when that bird shot his spear at me. How about that?"

Mike shrugged his heavy shoulders. "I'd guess there are three possibilities on that, Pete. One, the scuba diver thought you were a shark and shot at you in terror of his life. That's the most likely. Second, he was so startled at the sight of you that he shot before he realized what he was doing. Blind impulse. You were pretty startled yourself, you say. And third, it's perfectly possible that when he grabbed onto that rock on the bottom to hold himself against the surge of the swell, he jerked the trigger of his gun by mistake during his struggle to stay put. He didn't intend to shoot his gun at all. Much less at you. The thing just happened to be pointing your way at the time." Mike smiled suddenly, showing his big white teeth under his thin black mustache. "You got to remember, Pete, that the guy was only four or five feet away from you when the gun went off. According to your own story. If he'd been *trying* to spit you, he ought to have been able to do it at that range, oughtn't he?"

"Maybe not," I said. "I took off for the surface just as the missile was released. If I'd have been a second later, he'd have hit me."

"Well, I'm glad he didn't," Mike said heartily.

"Thanks," I said. "Thanks a lot. Then you don't think there's any tie-up between all these screwy incidents, as you call them, and Roscoe Chapin?"

"The chances are a hundred to one against it."

"But there *is* that one chance, all the same, isn't there?"

"Sure." Mike was brisk. "Here's something else to keep in mind, though. You *asked* for all these things that have been happening to you, Pete. You've been . . . snooping . . . haven't you?" He coughed. "Trespassing on other people's property? Aggressively messing around where you've no business to be. Right?"

"Well, I suppose you could call it that."

"I call it that. Figure it out for yourself, Pete. If you'd dated Susan What's-her-name in the regular way, and not gone fooling around Dolphin Inlet, none of this would have happened, would it?"

"It did happen, though, Mike. That guy shot at me, and it's a creepy feeling."

"Don't I know it?" Mike said with instant sympathy. "I've had a few scares like that myself."

I sighed. "We'll stay away from Dolphin Inlet from now on."

"You do that. And you'll find everything will be safe and peaceful." Mike looked at me. My face must have shown I wasn't entirely satisfied by his reassurances. He was quiet for a second, then he said, "You still think there's a chance it was this Roscoe Chapin character who shot that spear at you, don't you?"

I nodded.

Mike hesitated a minute, then leaned forward and lifted the telephone on his desk. He spoke into it. "Get me the Freebooter Motel, Edna. The office."

While he waited, he toyed with a pencil, tapping the desk. He said, "Since you're Gloria's brother, I've decided to give you the very best treatment we have, Pete." This was supposed to be a joke. I didn't think it was funny. "I'll go take a look at this Roscoe Chapin of yours, if you like. That make you and Susan feel better?"

"You bet!" I said, caught by surprise. "Gee, Mike . . . !"

His call came through. He asked the desk clerk at the Freebooter whether they had a Mr. Roscoe Chapin registered there as a guest. I could hear the clerk's reply. "Yes," she said. "In cottage eighteen. Shall I ring him?"

"Don't bother," Mike said easily. "I'll come out there and see him personally sometime in the next day or so."

"Who shall I say called him?" the clerk asked.

"Perdido Key Police," Mike said. The girl's gasp was audible even over the phone. Mike laughed. "Nothing to worry about, miss. Routine traffic inquiry." He hung up and turned to me. "Want to go along?"

"Now?"

"Why not? Get it over with. He won't be expecting me yet. And it'll relieve your mind quicker, eh?"

"Let's go," I said.

Mike left word with Edna where we'd be. We went out and got in his police cruiser. "Siren, Pete?" he teased me as we pulled away from headquarters.

I was suddenly uncomfortable. I felt foolish. I said, "No, for gosh sakes, Mike, no siren!"

It didn't take us long to cover the ten miles to the Freebooter. Mike turned in through the stand of royal palms that lined the drive to the office, and drove on until we saw the number 18 in black numerals over one of the cottage carports. As we went past Susan's cottage, twelve, I hoped I'd catch a glimpse of her, but no such luck. Her car was there, though. She and her mother were probably on the beach.

Mike stopped the cruiser in front of cottage eighteen and set his brake. I said, "His car's not here, Mike."

Mike shrugged. "Maybe I should have warned the desk girl not to mention my call."

"You think he's skipped?"

Mike grinned at me. "Not likely. Why should an innocent tourist take it on the lam just because a small town cop wants to ask him about a minor traffic violation?"

"Maybe he's not so innocent, after all!"

"We'll see." Mike pushed the doorbell of cottage eighteen. Nothing happened. We waited a minute or two, then Mike gave it another try. No action.

I looked around. A maid with clean sheets and towels in her hands was about to go into cottage twenty next door. I said to Mike, "Maybe that girl can tell us where Chapin is."

Mike walked over, smiling. His splendid appearance fixed the maid in her tracks. He said, "Do you do cottage eighteen, miss?"

"Yes," she said in an admiring murmur.

"Know Mr. Chapin, the occupant?"

"Just by sight. I've seen him several times when I've done his cottage."

"He doesn't answer his bell. And his car's not in the carport. He hasn't checked out and left, has he?"

She shook her head. "Not so far as I know. I just finished doing his cottage before you came. His stuff's still there."

"Oh, good," Mike said. "I wanted to ask him a couple of questions. I can do it some other time."

The maid's eyes got round with excitement at the thought of the police being interested in one of the Freebooter's guests. One of *her* guests. She clutched the sheets and towels tight against her. "What's Mr. Chapin done?" she asked.

Mike said, "Nothing important. We think he may have finessed a stop sign. Wherever he went, you didn't see him go, eh?"

"No, sir." She struggled with her curiosity, then asked timidly, "You sure that's all he's done? Ignored a stop sign?"

Mike looked at her. "Why?"

"I thought maybe he was leading a double life," the maid said. The way she said "double life," you could tell she'd been reading something like that in one of those confession magazines.

"What makes you think that?" Mike asked. "Does he act suspicious in any way?"

"Oh no!" She seemed sorry she'd raised the question now. "Mr. Chapin's a very nice man. Polite and generous and minds his own business."

"Then what's all this about a double life?" Mike asked her gently.

"Only that he didn't sleep in his bed last night," the maid informed us. "And a couple of other times in the three weeks he's been a guest here, I haven't had to touch his bed in the morning, because it wasn't slept in."

Mike laughed. "That's hardly a crime. I daresay he's got friends living around here with whom he spends an occasional night."

"Then why does he pay forty dollars a day to sleep *here?*" the maid said swiftly. "That's sinful extravagance, if you ask me!"

"It sure is," Mike agreed, "but it's none of our business if a man wants to throw his money away. Is it?"

Mike has that trick of keeping people off balance by

finishing a lot of his sentences with a question like that. The maid fell silent.

Mike said, "Well, thanks, miss, for your help. I'll drop in and see Mr. Chapin when he gets back. No hurry." He put a hand on my arm to turn me toward the police car, and lifted his trooper's hat politely to the maid. *"Adios,"* he said. Gloria told me that when Mike says good-by in Spanish like that, any girl would simply hate to see him leave, he sounds so romantic. I didn't think his Spanish did much for the maid. She just stood there, awkwardly, and watched us leave.

In the car, Mike started the motor and said to me, "We have nothing against Roscoe Chapin to warrant any investigation of him or any expenditure of official funds on him. Not even an infraction of traffic rules, Pete. Of course, I'll at least talk to him on the phone, and find out in short order whether he's your underwater marksman or not."

"How?" I asked.

"Question of alibi," Mike said. "I'll ask him where he was when the man shot at you yesterday. He tells me. Can he prove it, I ask him. He says certainly, and names witnesses or something that will back him up. I check out the alibi, find it holds up and bingo! We know the guy with the speargun was John Q. Tourist maybe, but not Roscoe Chapin. Then you can stop worrying about the guy. Check?"

I was convinced. "Check, Mike," I said. "And thanks for taking all this trouble today. Sorry I bothered you."

He punched my shoulder. "Forget it. Any brother of Gloria's will soon be a brother of mine!" He began to whistle. We rolled toward the highway.

I looked ahead through the windshield as we followed the motel drive past the scattered cottages. I said, "Hold it!"

"What now?" He slowed down.

"That's Susan Frost in front of cottage twelve, flagging us down," I told him. "The girl who was with me at Dolphin Inlet . . . "

"Oh, yeah. I'll be glad to meet her. Your sister says she's quite a dish." He brought the cruiser to a halt beside Susan, who was standing on the edge of the drive and making semaphoring motions with her arms. She had on jeans and a shirt that was too big for her by four sizes. She looked great.

"Pete!" she said as we pulled up. "I *thought* that was you I saw in this car when you went by our window a few minutes ago."

Mike and I got out and I introduced him to Susan. She gave him a smile and said, "Oh, I've heard a lot about you, Officer Sebastien!" and the way she said it made Mike grin at me. Susan went on, "And what did you find out about Roscoe Chapin at cottage eighteen, Pete? I saw you stop there."

I told her we'd found out nothing. Except that Chapin had slept out last night. And I told her that Mike thought we were away out in left field with our suspicions of Chapin, anyway. She could hardly wait until I finished to say, "Well, *I've* found out something that I think is kind of sinister, officer!"

"Oh?" Mike murmured, all politeness.

"Yes. I just happened to be talking with one of the bellboys here at the Freebooter who helps you unload your bags

and things when you arrive, you know?" "Just happened!"
I wondered about that.

Mike nodded. "You said sinister," he kidded her. "What
did you learn from this bellboy that was sinister?"

Susan took a deep breath. "He just happened to be the
bellboy who helped Mr. Chapin unload his luggage when
he checked in here three weeks ago," Susan said. "And
guess what? The bellboy said that Mr. Chapin had a lot
of scuba diving gear in the trunk of his car, along with his
bags!"

She looked at me when she made this announcement to
see if I was impressed. I was. But not Mike.

"Is that the sinister part, Susan?" he said.

"Why, of course! After all, it proves Roscoe Chapin is
a scuba diver, doesn't it? And so it was probably Mr. Chapin who shot that spear at Pete yesterday! What could be
plainer than that?" She was excited.

"Whoa, whoa," Mike soothed her. "That's no kind of
legal proof, Susan. None at all. Thousands of tourists carry
scuba gear in their trunks. You know that. Skin and scuba
diving isn't as big as surfing down here now, but it's still
big!"

"Yes, but not very likely at Dolphin Inlet!" Susan answered. "Roscoe Chapin would be the only scuba diver
aside from the Osgoods who might be diving at a private
place like Dolphin Inlet."

"And Pete," Mike said mildly. "*He* was diving there. And
what about that mysterious man you call Mr. X? I gathered
from Pete's story that *he* might be diving there, too."

Susan's eyes began to shoot sparks. She said to Mike,

"You're not taking this seriously! Pete was nearly killed yesterday and here you are, making a joke of it!"

That shook him a little. I couldn't help laughing. "That's telling him, Susan," I cheered her on.

"Now wait a minute!" Mike protested. "I'm trying to help you kids. You must see that. But I can't help you unless you're willing to be reasonable. I just promised Pete I'd check out Mr. Chapin very carefully."

"When?" asked Susan.

"Whenever I can get in touch with him."

"That might be next week sometime!"

"Listen, Mike," I said, "Susan's got a point, hasn't she? Chapin hasn't come back here since yesterday. So maybe he'll *never* come back."

Mike raised his eyebrows. "His stuff's still here."

"Sure. But what if that *was* Roscoe Chapin I met underwater yesterday? And what if he drowned in Dolphin Inlet?"

"Oh!" Susan said.

Mike said, "That's a bare possibility, I suppose. You said he was in trouble the last you saw of him. And the storm was blowing up."

"Yeah," I said eagerly. "And there's one thing that might tell us whether Chapin really went to Dolphin Inlet yesterday."

"What's that?"

"His car."

"How do you figure? His car's missing, too."

"That's right," I said, lining up my idea. "Look, Dolphin Inlet's a good five miles from here, right? If Chapin wanted to do any diving there, he'd certainly not try to swim all the way from here. The natural thing to do would be to drive in his rented car to some place close to Dolphin Inlet. Right?"

"Of course." This was Susan.

"And you think if he drowned or is still at the inlet we ought to be able to find his car somewhere close by, is that it?" Mike said.

"Sure. Doesn't that make sense?"

Mike grinned. "In a kind of a knot-headed way, I guess." He got back into the police cruiser. "All right. I give up. Come on, kids, we'll have a quick look for Chapin's car at Dolphin Inlet. Then will you be satisfied?"

While I got in beside Mike, Susan ran for her car under the carport of cottage twelve. "I'll follow you!" she called. "I can't bear to miss this!"

10

THE GOLDEN DOUBLOON

I was so sure we'd find Roscoe Chapin's car parked somewhere near Dolphin Inlet that I was in a real hurry to get there, but Mike kept the speed of his patrol car down to a measly thirty-five miles an hour. The limit on Perdido Key is forty, and I had a hunch Mike was crawling along that way just to keep me on edge.

I said, "Can't we pour on a little coal, Mike? We haven't got all day. I'm supposed to be working."

"So am I." He looked at me out of the corner of his eye. "There's no hurry, Pete. If his car's there, it's there. And it won't run away . . . especially if he drowned yesterday. Right?"

"Yes, but . . . "

"And if Roscoe Chapin does decide to head home in his car at this very coincidental minute," Mike went on, "he'll have to pass us to get there, won't he? And we'll meet him." He glanced at his rearview mirror. "That girl friend of yours is going to get a summons for tailgating, Pete, if she doesn't drop back a little."

I looked back, and the nose of Susan's Chevy was practically in our back seat. I laughed. "I guess she's in a hurry to get there, too."

Mike said, "Why are you wasting your time on Roscoe Chapin and Dolphin Inlet when she's around?"

"That's what Pop asked me. I don't know, Mike. Honest. Except the whole thing's kind of got my curiosity up, and we're both pretty mad at whoever it was who scared us that night in the woods and shot at me with a speargun yesterday."

Mike nodded. "I can understand that." He began to slow down. "We're two miles north of Dolphin Inlet here. So start keeping your eye peeled for that rental job Chapin is driving. Dark sedan, license 16E–714, wasn't that it?"

"Yeah." I began to scan both sides of Gulf Road and the occasional houses that bordered it here very carefully. I checked the license number of every car we passed on the road or saw standing in driveways or carports along the way. "I think it'll be closer to the inlet than this," I said.

"I do, too. If it's here at all. Might as well be thorough, though. Lucky for us it's so easy."

"What do you mean, easy?"

"Only place the car can be is along Gulf Road, one side or the other. For this is the only road, right?"

"But there's a lot of driveways and lanes from houses and . . ."

Mike shook his head. "Not near Dolphin Inlet, Pete. Nothing but woods on both sides of the road. You know that. No roads in them, either."

"Anyway, the car's got to be here somewhere," I said stubbornly. "If it's not parked on the edge of the road . . ."

"And it's not. We'd have seen it when we drove to the Freebooter, wouldn't we?"

". . . then it's hidden in the woods some place," I finished lamely.

"How? In those woods? There isn't any way you can drive a car a hundred feet into them from Gulf Road. At least, not without leaving a trail of broken palmettos and brush we could spot a mile away."

"Well, let's look anyway, Mike. We're nearly there now." Some way ahead, I could see the two cabbage palms beside the road that Susan and I had been using for a parking landmark on our visits to the inlet. And that's all I could see. As far as my eye could reach southward on Gulf Road, there was absolutely no sign of a car parked on either side of it.

"You look under the trees on your side, I'll look on mine," Mike said. He slowed to a crawl. "Sing out if you see anything looks like a car."

Susan wasn't following so closely now. She had dropped back and was turning her head from side to side as she drove very slowly. She was searching for Chapin's car, too.

When we'd gone two miles south of the Dolphin Inlet area, Mike pulled up. He could see I was disappointed, and there was a note of sympathy in his voice.

"We'll make one more pass over the road each way, Pete, shall we? Just to be sure? It'll only take a few minutes."

"Thanks, Mike," I answered. "I guess it wouldn't do any good." Susan pulled up behind us. She stuck her head out of the window and called to me, "Did you see any sign of the car?"

"Nope. Did you?"

"No." She sounded let down. "What'll we do now?"

I didn't answer her. I turned to Mike and said, "I don't suppose you'd want to make a call on the Osgoods, would you?"

"What for?"

"To look them over, kind of. Especially Mr. X. The way you were going to look over Roscoe Chapin?"

Mike shook his head. "No excuse in the world to go barging in there, Pete. Nobody in the inlet's done anything out of line, far's I can see. Now, if it had been one of the Osgoods or Mr. X tried to shoot you . . . "

"I was afraid you'd say that. Oh, well." I climbed out of the patrol car.

"Where you going?"

"I'll ride back to the market with Susan," I told him. "Then you can go straight back to headquarters. Thanks, Mike, for trying to help us figure out Roscoe Chapin. I hope he's not drowned, that's all."

"I imagine he'll turn up safe and sound. And I'll check his alibi, if any, for that speargun attack on you. That's about as far as I can go now. Unless you want me to ride this road again."

"Never mind," I said. "Susan and I'll take one more look. There's no reason to waste your time, though. Thanks again."

He waved a hand and pulled away. "Any time," he said.

I walked back to Susan's car, opened the front door and

got in beside her. "Darn the luck!" she said. "I was *sure* we'd see some sign of the car!"

I gave her a big grin. "You're a better cop than Mike. At least you've got more persistence. And more faith in my hunches."

She began to turn the car. "Let's take one more look," she suggested.

"Fine. That's what I hoped you'd want to do. Because I do, too. And by the way, can you drive me back to work afterward? I told Mike you would, so he'd leave. If you're busy . . . "

"If I'm busy, you'll *walk* the five miles home, and get there just in time to close up shop for the day, is that it?"

I had the grace to stutter a little. "Well," I said, "yes, I suppose so. See, I wanted to talk to you for a few minutes without Mike. . . . "

"What about?" she asked innocently.

"About how smart you were to find out that Roscoe Chapin had scuba gear in his car trunk."

"Oh. That was easy. And kind of fun. I was so mad at whoever shot at you under the Gulf yesterday that I got a kick out of trying to find out who it was."

"Well, thanks, Susan. Mike doesn't think it means anything—what you found out—but I do." I admired her profile for a second. Then I said, "So let's find that rented car of Chapin's if we can, okay?"

"All right. And in answer to your question, Pete"—she looked sideways at me—"of course I'll drive you home. I have nothing to do until Daddy arrives at Sarta City Airport at half-past twelve. I'm going to meet his plane from here. So I'll drop you off on my way."

"Where's your mother?" I asked.

"She's having her hair done."

"Great," I said. "I forgot your father's due in today."

"You'll like him."

Slowly she cruised northward on Gulf Road and we gave both sides of the highway another careful inspection without any more luck that we had the first time.

A quarter-mile beyond the cabbage palms, Susan suddenly tramped on her power brakes. I nearly went through the windshield. "Look at that!" she said, pointing dramatically out of the window on her side.

I craned my neck to look past her. "What?"

"Don't you see it? That entrance to a track or lane of some kind . . . all overgrown?"

She was right. Just beyond the gravel shoulder of the road a kind of flat, grassy patch of sand made a slight indentation in the line of woods. It was so overgrown with weeds and ground-hugging vegetation that you'd hardly know it was there. I peered into the woods and saw that there seemed to be an opening through the trees and scrub away from the old track entrance Susan had spotted.

"Hey!" I said. "The demon detective! You've done it again!"

She hurriedly pulled her car over to the left side of the road. We jumped out. "Doesn't it look as though that could be what's left of an old lane or something?" she asked.

"It sure does. One that hasn't been used for years, by the look of it." I bent down and squinted at the low growth of grass and weeds. I felt excitement build inside me. "Here's something that *could* have been made by an auto tire, Susan! See this mark?"

She bent and looked where I pointed, her hair falling forward past her cheeks. "Yes!" she said. "It is! Come on, Pete! I bet we'll find Chapin's car in here!"

She reached out and grabbed my hand and held it tightly as we plunged into the woods along the faintly marked ancient track. The vicinity of Dolphin Inlet seemed to make her nervous, for which I was glad, if it meant holding hands with her.

We made fast progress. Around us, trees and bushes smothered the old path we followed almost completely, but not quite. There was still room for an automobile to negotiate the track if driven slowly and carefully over potholes and windfalls and between trees. And evidently one had passed this way several times lately. For we found other tire marks as we went deeper into the woods and the ground grew softer.

The track appeared to me to bend slightly south and west as we followed it hand in hand. Occasionally we could see the deep-blue sky, barred with long fleecy clouds, above us through the trees. And after we'd gone maybe five hundred yards, the reflection of sunlight on the open Gulf suddenly made a bright shimmer ahead of us.

"Where do you suppose we are?" Susan spoke in a tense whisper as though she was afraid somebody might be listening.

"About opposite the end of Dolphin Point," I calculated, "figuring from the way this track has bent. Across the inlet from the Osgoods' house. On the northern point of the inlet crescent, maybe. This must have been an old logging road, or one that led to some oyster beds on the north shore of the inlet years ago . . . "

Susan said, "Now who's the detective? Here's a pile of oyster shells."

And there they were, several piles of old shells among the trees, almost hidden by creepers. I started to say something, I forget what, because just then Susan said in a sort of squeak, "There it is!" and nearly pinched my hand off, she squeezed it so hard.

I looked ahead and saw the looming shape of an automobile silhouetted against the brightness of the Gulf.

The car was parked where the old track petered out in a small clearing inside the wooded north edge of Dolphin Inlet. It was far enough back from the narrow beach that bordered the inlet on this side to be nearly concealed from any curious eyes in the inlet itself.

My own curious eyes, once I'd taken in the situation, went like striking snakes to the license plate on the rear of the automobile. Susan was ahead of me, of course, because she was already reading the license number out loud. "16E–714."

It was Roscoe Chapin's car.

Cautiously we drew nearer. She didn't let go of my hand. Pretty soon we could make out that the windows were all closed. And the doors were locked, as we found out when we tried to open them. The car was absolutely empty.

"Never mind, Susan," I said. I was whispering now, myself. There was something pretty oppressive about that quiet deserted car hidden among the trees. "We know it's Chapin's car. And we know he's not in it."

"The trunk?" Susan whispered.

I shivered in spite of myself. "Cut it out!" I managed to blurt. I wasn't at all sure that Roscoe Chapin might not be curled inside that locked trunk listening to every word we said.

I hoped he wasn't, though, because the next thing Susan said was, "Then it *was* Roscoe Chapin who shot that spear at you, Pete!"

I nodded. There didn't seem much doubt about it now. I pulled her forward until we were past the car and standing at the edge of the woods. Five yards ahead of us, a kind of low sand dune made a little hump between us and the water's edge. I remembered there had been a narrow beach here yesterday; last night's storm, however, had sent wild water crashing ashore here that had wiped out the beach and badly undercut the sand dune itself.

As my eyes went out across the water toward the inlet mouth, Susan whispered "Look, Pete," and pointed to a single line of dimples in the sand at our feet. They led from where we crouched to the lip of the sand dune before us. They were nearly filled with blown sand now, yet there wasn't any doubt what they were. Or whose they were. Roscoe Chapin's footprints.

"Only one set," Susan said.

"He went into the water here. But he didn't come out here," I said. I pointed in my turn. "Look out there."

Not more than a hundred yards away, the Osgoods' specimen boat was anchored outside the inlet's mouth. The

Gulf was still choppy from last night's storm, so the specimen boat was moving around over its anchor. For a few seconds, the deckhouse hid most of the boat's deck from us; then the water worked it around enough for us to catch a quick impression of somebody leaning over the low rail on the boat's starboard side.

"There's somebody on it," I said. We were back to whispering again. We watched for another shift in the boat's position so we could see more. Temporarily the deckhouse again blanked things out for us. That's when something occurred to me that I should have thought of sooner. If we could see the Osgoods' boat out there so plain and make out a man on it, there was no reason why the man on the boat, whoever he was, couldn't see Susan and me just as plain if he happened to look in our direction. We were standing in full view at the edge of the woods, elevated two or three feet above sea level.

I grabbed Susan's arm and pulled her down into a crouch. "He'll see us if he looks this way. Let's crawl behind that sand dune up ahead, shall we? If we lie on our stomachs, we can peek over it and be pretty well hidden from the boat."

"Okay," Susan agreed instantly. "Lead the way."

I got down on my stomach and wormed my way quickly to the sheltering sand dune. It was only seven or eight feet. Then I kept my head down and turned to motion to Susan. She followed me, flat on her stomach, wriggling forward as cool as a platoon sergeant on jungle patrol. When we were lying side by side behind the dune, we cautiously lifted our heads until our eyes topped the sand ridge.

It wasn't long until the currents shifted the boat broadside to us, and we could make out the figure on the deck more clearly.

In my ear, Susan whispered, "It's Perry Osgood. Tall and thin . . ."

"Yeah." I nodded and got sand in my mouth for my trouble.

"What's he doing?"

"Hauling up something, looks like. On a hand line."

As we watched, a round hand basket came out of the Gulf at the end of Perry's rope, and was lifted carefully over the rail, leaking water in streams. Perry immediately squatted down on his heels and began to stir the basket's contents about with his fingers, as though he was looking for something.

"Specimens," Susan said.

"Mr. X or Hamilton Osgood must be down on the bottom, filling the basket for him. Watch the boarding ladder amidships. Maybe he'll come up."

Susan didn't take her eyes off the specimen boat. Neither did I. All at once Susan whispered, "What if Roscoe *Chapin's* down there filling Perry's baskets?"

That was one possibility I hadn't thought of. "Keep watching."

Almost as I said the words, a black-clad figure with compressed air cylinders on its back bobbed up beside the boat. The diver reached with one hand for the aluminum boarding ladder. With the other, he pushed up his face mask.

I shifted my position a bit on the brink of our sand dune and lifted myself on my elbows to get a better look at the diver's face.

That did it.

Almost my full weight rested on my elbows for a second. And my elbows were supported by the undercut lip of the little sand dune. They sank into the sand and a ten-inch section of the dune's seaward overhang crumbled and broke away. The dislodged sand slid slowly down into the water of Dolphin Inlet at the base of the dune.

I scrambled to keep from sliding after it, and managed to anchor myself again beside Susan.

Susan hadn't noticed. She said, "It's Mr. X, Pete! The diver is Mr. X!"

I was about to take a look at the diver myself when a gleam caught my eyes in the sand. It wasn't six inches from my nose—where my elbows had dislodged the crescent-shaped wedge of dune top. It looked like the glint of sun on metal. Like the glint of sun on gold, in fact.

I reached for it, plucked it from the wet sand it was half buried in. Holding it in one palm, I brushed grains of sand off its surface with my fingers. Wondering why I wasn't saying anything, Susan turned her eyes my way. "'What's that thing, Pete?" she whispered curiously.

I knew what it was now. It was about the size of a silver dollar and where I'd cleaned the sand off it, the shield-shaped coat of arms came up clear. Also the date: 1714. And even the letters that spelled out Philippus V around the edge.

In a voice that sounded funny to me, I said, "It's a Spanish doubloon, Susan. A gold doubloon."

She forgot to whisper. "A doubloon! Are you sure, Pete?" She reached for it. "How do you know?"

I raised my eyes to the specimen boat in the mouth of

Dolphin Inlet and the truth hit me like a ton of mullet pouring from a tipped net. I said, "I just know it, that's all. And I know something else, too. Finally."

"What?"

"I know what Perry Osgood and Mr. X are diving for out there, Susan. Not marine specimens or bottom samples or anything like that. They're diving for sunken treasure!"

11 ✿

A QUESTION OF LAW

We backed away from the sand dune fast, wriggling flat to avoid being seen by Perry Osgood or Mr. X. Inside the border of the woods, I helped Susan to her feet and we skirted Chapin's deserted car and made for Gulf Road up the overgrown track.

For several minutes, neither of us said a word. We were too stunned, I guess. Yet neither of us doubted for a second that we'd stumbled on the truth of the queer goings-on in Dolphin Inlet.

We were both natives of Florida, remember, born and raised in the state. And where kids from other states might have failed to make a quick connection between the golden doubloon I'd found and sunken treasure in Dolphin Inlet, it was the only explanation that made sense to Susan and me.

We were both familiar with the many stories of treasure finds along the Florida coastline—the discovery of Spanish plate ships, sunk more than two centuries ago in the coastal waters of Florida by great storms while carrying the treasure of the New World back to Spain. And we both knew, from newspaper reports, that so many old Spanish coins, washed out of sunken treasure hulks by modern storms, had been found on Florida beaches recently by casual beach-walkers that they hardly made conversation any more. So when you put my doubloon, found on an undercut beach after a severe storm, together with secret diving activity less than a hundred yards away, you couldn't miss it. Especially when the Osgoods seemed so allergic to intruders.

After we'd walked a little way, Susan stopped dead still in the middle of the track. "You mean there's a Spanish treasure ship sunk at Dolphin Inlet, don't you?" she said quietly. "Out there where they're diving?"

I said, "It's hard to believe. But it must be so, Susan."

She nodded solemnly. "If this was St. Augustine or Vero Beach or Fort Pierce or some place on the east coast, I'd believe it, Pete. But Perdido Key! On the west coast?"

I knew what she was worrying about. Every Florida schoolboy knows the route of the Spanish treasure fleets lay from Havana through the Straits of Florida and up our east coast. Just north of the Bahamas, the ships usually turned eastward across the Atlantic for Spain. To find a treasure ship off Florida's east coast was almost common-place, now; the *west* coast was something new and differ-ent. I said, "A king-size hurricane must have caught this baby about Key West and driven her up the west coast this far before she sank."

"If there's a treasure ship at Dolphin Inlet," Susan said, beginning to move forward again, "no wonder the Osgoods and Mr. X are acting so funny! And trying to keep out snoopers!"

I quickened my pace to keep up with her. "No wonder at all," I said. "If people around here realized there was sunken treasure in Dolphin Inlet, the entire population of Perdido Key and Sarta City would be out here in a flash, bumper to bumper, standing in line to get into Dolphin Inlet. Or to cut in on the treasure. You can't blame the Osgoods for trying to guard their privacy."

"Heavens, no. They'd be swamped with tourists."

I was thinking straighter now that the surprise of discovery was fading. "If they've got a treasure-hunting license from the state," I said, "they wouldn't have much to worry about, though. Their salvage rights would be protected . . . " Another thought hit me. "Hey! What if they *don't* have a treasure-hunting license? What if they haven't reported to the state that they've located this treasure?"

Susan and I both knew that the state of Florida issues treasure-hunting licenses and that you have to give the state twenty-five per cent of any treasure you salvage. Susan said, "I bet they're keeping their treasure secret so they won't have to give a quarter of it to the state!"

I nodded. "That could be. And maybe that's why they're trying so hard to make everybody think they're marine researchers—so they'll have a ready-made excuse for all the diving they do."

We reached Gulf Road and went over to where Susan's car was parked and got in. She didn't start the engine right away. She pulled down the sun visor over her seat and looked in the mirror that was fixed on the back of it. "Look at me!" she said. "I'm an awful mess! Covered with dirt and sand. And I've ripped off a button crawling on my stomach like that!"

I said the right thing for a change. I said, "Mess or not, you look great to me!"

She pushed her hair back from her forehead and forgot about the mirror. "Exactly what *are* you supposed to do about a treasure ship when you find one?" she asked then.

I shrugged. "I've never found one, so I'm not sure. All I know is that the state gets twenty-five per cent of what you bring up, or else you're in trouble. That's why you're supposed to apply for a license to hunt for treasure and salvage it. So the state can keep track of what you're doing and sort of supervise the whole business."

"Then we ought to tell Mr. Sebastien about the Osgoods' treasure right away, don't you think?"

I didn't say anything for a minute. I was thinking about how I'd feel if I'd found a sunken treasure ship in the bayou behind our fish market. Finally I said, "I'm not real sure I want to tell the police, Susan."

"Why not? If it's against the law, what they're doing in Dolphin Inlet . . . "

"Well, wait a minute. If *I* found a sunken ship full of treasure and invested a lot of dough in boats and diving equipment, and even bought the property near where the treasure ship was sunk so I could salvage it easier, I'd hate to have to fork over a quarter of all the stuff I found to the state, wouldn't you? Just because a bunch of Congressmen and lawyers or somebody up in Tallahassee said so?"

"I'm from Tallahassee myself, Pete. And Daddy's a lawyer, remember? So what can I say?"

I laughed. "Nothing personal, Susan. Only I think I'd rather let the Osgoods hang onto all the treasure they can bring up than tip off the cops that they're maybe gypping the state."

"Why, Pete, you're completely irresponsible!" She smiled her crooked smile at me. "And yet . . . I feel a little bit the same way myself."

"Anyway, they're probably just trying to keep claim jumpers and hijackers out of their hair."

"I bet *that's* what he is," Susan said.

"Who?"

"Roscoe Chapin! He's a crook! That's why he's been spying on the Osgoods and Dolphin Inlet. He knows about the treasure ship!"

Leave it to Susan to come up with the answers. I thought she was probably right. It would explain why Chapin had been wandering in Dolphin Inlet woods and diving at the inlet itself. I said, "We've already told Mike about Chapin. And he gave us a quick brush. Even if Chapin's a claim jumper or a hijacker, he still hasn't done anything Mike can pinch him for."

"How about the Osgoods and Mr. X, then?"

"We just decided their treasure is none of our business, didn't we?"

Susan turned the ignition key and the starter whirred. We started south toward Fiesta Village.

We watched the road ahead of us, both too busy thinking about Dolphin Inlet and what lay on the Gulf bottom there to say anything more for a couple of miles.

Then Susan tossed her hair and gave me a look. "You know something, Pete?" she said. "We've found out *part* of what's happening at the inlet, about the treasure ship, but there's still some pretty sinister stuff going on there that we don't understand a bit."

"You mean like who is Mr. X? And where is Hamilton Osgood? Sure. All the more reason for not telling Mike Sebastien anything more. I already asked him those two questions, and he brushed them off, too."

"Then what'll we do, Pete?"

"Keep an eye on the inlet ourselves is all I can think of," I said, winking at her because I knew how much she was enjoying this local mystery of ours, the city girl on a country vacation.

She had a different idea. "Listen. Daddy is going to be here in an hour. He's a lawyer. He knows a lot of government people in Tallahassee. And he'll know all about the treasure-hunting laws in Florida, I'm pretty sure. So why don't we tell *him* about Dolphin Inlet and see what *he* says we should do?"

I went for that, hook, line and sinker. "Susan," I said, "you're not only a painter, a detective and a good-looking bird, but a good *thinker,* too! Only one thing. *You'll* have to tell your father about Dolphin Inlet. Because if I take any more time away from my job at the fish market, Gloria will skin and fillet me with a dull knife and feed me to the cat!"

12 ✺

SUNKEN TREASURE

I didn't hear what Susan's father thought about Dolphin Inlet until the next morning.

I was scaling four speckled trout (they're called weakfish up North) when the phone in the fish market rang and Gloria, who was waiting on Mrs. Haggerty, answered it. She got that look in her eye and said, "Hoo-hoo, Pete! It's for you. Guess who?" She didn't even muffle the receiver.

I grabbed the phone from her without waiting to rinse the fish scales off my hands, and said, "Hello?"

"Pete?" It was Susan.

"Yeah, Susan," I answered in a low voice. "Don't mind my sister's kidding." I gave Gloria a mean look.

"I'm used to it," Susan said. "Daddy teases me about everybody who so much as looks at me. He's been needling me about *you* ever since he arrived and I told him about Dolphin Inlet. Anyway, what I wanted to tell you, Mr. Simons in Tallahassee just called Daddy back a few minutes ago . . ."

"Mr. Simons?"

"Yes. He's a friend of Daddy's who's a trustee of the Florida Internal Improvement Fund."

"Oh. You said he called your father back. Does that mean your father called him first?"

"Of course. Last night."

"Wait a minute," I said. "Break it down for me. First, what did your father think about our Dolphin Inlet story?" I looked over my shoulder. "Make it fast, Susan. Mrs. Haggerty is waiting for her trout."

"Oh! Well, I told Daddy everything yesterday. And he said right away that probably the Osgoods and Mr. X are carrying on a perfectly legitimate salvage operation. *If* there's really a sunken Spanish treasure ship there at all. He thinks that's possible, but not probable."

"It's there," I said. I hadn't a doubt about that.

"Anyway," Susan went on, "Daddy said before we get all excited about it, the obvious thing to do was check up on the Osgoods and find out for sure whether they *had* a treasure-hunting license and had reported their treasure find to the state."

I said, "Hold it a minute, and let me finish Mrs. Haggerty's fish. I'll be back in a flash." I put the phone down and went over to the cleaning table and finished Mrs. Haggerty's trout, because she was beginning to shuffle her feet and pretend to cough the way a lot of women do to show their impatience. Gloria wasn't paying her much attention, either, for Gloria was openly listening to my end of the telephone conversation. When Mrs. Haggerty left with her fish, I got back on the phone.

"Susan? So your father called this Mr. Simons and asked him to check in Tallahassee, is that it?"

"Yes. And Mr. Simons said he would. And he did. This morning, first thing. And he just called back. There's absolutely no record in the files of a treasure-hunting license being issued to anyone named Osgood. And no treasure find has been reported by anybody from Perdido Key."

"Well," I said. "Then that leaves us where?"

"Daddy thinks the same as you did, Pete. That maybe the Osgoods and Mr. X are keeping their treasure hunting quiet to fend off curiosity-seekers and robbers."

I grunted. I said, "So what's your father think we ought to do? Anything?"

Susan laughed. "Oh, yes, his call created a good deal of curiosity in Tallahassee as you can imagine, and the Internal Improvement Fund is sending Mr. Simons down here to Perdido Key today on a plane. Another man named Professor Harris is coming, too. He's from the Florida State Museum in Gainesville."

I felt a twinge of uneasiness. If the state was sending an investigator to Dolphin Inlet, and a professor along with him . . . "What's he a professor of?" I asked Susan.

"Underwater archaeology, or something like that."

"Uh-huh," I said. The official wheels were really beginning to roll. My feeling of uneasiness got worse, because I knew I was responsible for the whole thing. Susan and I, that is. And here were the authorities charging down to Perdido Key on the basis of nothing but an informed guess on the part of a couple of kids. I didn't like it.

Susan was talking again. "So Daddy wants to know if you

won't come to supper at our cottage tonight, Pete. He wants to talk to you about Dolphin Inlet. And so do Mr. Simons and Professor Harris. And they want to see the gold doubloon you found yesterday. You can come, can't you?"

"I-I guess so," I said. "What time?" I was thinking that I'd finish work at six and I'd have to take time for a good shower to kill the fish smell. . . .

"Seven o'clock?"

"Okay. I'll be there."

"Good. Isn't it all terribly exciting, Pete?" She gave her musical laugh.

I said, "It sure is. All I hope is, we're right about the treasure ship, Susan. Otherwise, we're dead!" I hung up.

We didn't have dinner in the Frosts' cottage after all, because Mrs. Frost thought it was too cramped for six people to eat in their little dinette, so we had a fancy dinner at the Freebooter Restaurant and went to the Frosts' cottage afterward to talk.

All the decorations in the restaurant are pirate stuff, and the waiters wear pirate costumes and one gold earring each, and the prices on the menu are in pieces of eight instead of dollars. I ordered a New York cut steak, medium, before I found out what a piece of eight was worth and that my steak was going to cost Mr. Frost over six bucks in American money! I was too embarrassed to change my order. Anyway, the steak was delicious. Susan ordered scallops and I was glad to see they were the real article. Sometimes you order scallops and what you get is lumps of dog shark meat instead. Most people can't tell the difference.

Susan's father was a shortish man with red hair and a big tough-looking jaw. His chin had a hollow in the middle of it and his eyes kind of pinned you to the wall when he looked at you.

His friend, Mr. Simons, the trustee from the Improvement Fund, was round and fat and bald and used two-dollar words a lot. The first joint of his ring finger was missing and I wondered whether he'd lost it cleaning fish, maybe, when he was young.

Professor Harris was built like a pro football tackle. The Dolphins should have one like him. But he wore thick glasses that made his eyes look enormous. He told me he'd had cataracts, and that he'd had diving goggles made with that same thick prescription glass in them because he did a lot of diving in connection with his work.

Well, when we went back to the Frosts' cottage after we'd finished eating, Mrs. Frost had us all sit down and brought out some little cups of after-dinner coffee and passed them around. Then Mr. Frost asked me to tell them in detail everything I knew or guessed about Dolphin Inlet and all the odd things that had happened to me and Susan there.

I did the best I could.

When I came to the part about finding the doubloon, I took it out of my pocket and passed it to Professor Harris. He took one look at it through his thick glasses, front and back, and tossed it to Mr. Simons. "It's genuine," he said. "No question about it. Spanish doubloon minted in Mexico City in 1714." He looked at me and grinned. "In terms of our money, Pete, your doubloon was probably worth over a hundred dollars when it was struck in 1714. But plenty of coin collectors will pay you up to a thousand dollars for it today."

"Wow!" Susan piped up. "You're rich, Pete!"

Her father shushed her and I finished telling them about Dolphin Inlet. Mr. and Mrs. Frost had already heard most of it from Susan; Mr. Simons and Professor Harris listened to every word.

At the end, Mr. Simons said, "How's it sound to you, Max?" Max was Professor Harris. "Myself, I'd say that not only have Pete's actions in this matter been exceptionally circumspect, but his analysis of the situation admirably plausible. I'll go further. I'm willing to hazard the firm opinion that there's a Spanish hulk on the bottom of the Gulf at Dolphin Inlet, exactly as Pete and Susan have envisaged it."

Professor Harris moved his head up and down in a nod. "Me, too," he said briskly. "Sounds like the kids have earned the thanks of your people, Frank. I agree that on the evidence so far, it seems pretty likely that there's a Spanish treasure ship at this Dolphin Inlet place. Although heaven knows how it happened to sink away up here on the west coast!"

Susan spoke up. "Pete thinks a hurricane must have caught a plate fleet somewhere around Key West, and a crazy wind of some kind cut this ship out of the fleet and drove it north up the west coast onto the rocks at the base of Dolphin Point."

Professor Harris said, "Not a bad guess, Pete. It's the

only way it could have happened, I dare say. This is the first treasure find I've heard about on the west coast, but that doesn't mean it couldn't happen."

Mr. Simons laughed. "Matter of fact," he said, "we have an investigator looking into a reported treasure find down around Fort Myers right this minute. Fellow down there's supposed to have unearthed some solid gold Aztec statuettes. So Dolphin Inlet won't be the initial west coast find."

"About this diving that's going on in the inlet," Professor Harris said. "Three people, or possibly four, if we count this Hamilton Osgood you haven't seen yet, hardly seem enough hands to do an efficient job of underwater salvage, Pete. The treasure hunts I'm familiar with on the east coast are usually pretty well-staffed, scientific undertakings, aren't they, Frank?"

"Of course," Simons answered. "But they're overt ventures, properly accredited and licensed by the state, and officially protected against piratical attacks during salvage, if any. This thing here, on the other hand . . ."

When he paused, Mr. Frost spoke for the first time. ". . . is quite evidently clandestine in the extreme," he said. "Under the circumstances, you couldn't expect it to be anything else. And I guess there's no reason why two or three skillful divers can't clean out a treasure wreck pretty handily, is there? It just takes them longer than it would a bigger group, I should think."

"That's right," Professor Harris said. "And their equipment described by Pete just now—the two boats and the diving gear—sounds quite adequate to me."

I got up nerve enough to ask, "What was that thing like a vacuum cleaner, sir? They said it was used to suck up samples of bottom."

"They were telling the truth," said the professor, "up to a point. That dredging apparatus is probably being used to suck up sand on the Gulf bottom in one place and move it to another spot."

Simons nodded agreement. "That's always the vital factor in treasure salvage from sunken ships, Pete," he said. He talked more like a professor than the professor did. "It is essential to move sand—quantities of it—from one place to another on the sea bottom."

"Why?" asked Susan. "I should think you'd just go down and pick up what treasure you could see and . . ."

"There's more to it than that, my dear," Simons said. "Vastly more. You must understand that during the years since the ship sank, its wooden timbers have all either rotted away or been devoured by teredo worms, who have a voracious appetite for wood." He coughed. "You rarely see much treasure lying about on the sand in the open near the wreck. Occasionally a few coins or jewels that may have been washed into the open by the currents of strong storms, just as Pete's doubloon was undoubtedly washed ashore the other day. However, after the timbers are gone, about all that's left of the boat is a pile of ballast stones on the bottom, under which most of the valuable metal objects that were in the original ship lie buried. The ballast stones themselves get partially covered with sand as well. Thus, if you wish to recover treasure in any worthwhile amount, you must first move the ballast stones that lie over it. And to do that, it is absolutely imperative that you move tons and tons of sand. Is that clear?"

"Sure," I said. "But how does that dredge of theirs move sand?"

Professor Harris said, "They probably pump hose water at high pressure into the open-ended pipe and start suction so the sea rushes in, pulling sand with it. And small objects, too, like coins. The sand, shells and small stuff it sucks up come out of the pipe a few feet away and settle to the bottom there where they can be easily examined for any little bits of treasure they contain. And meanwhile, a lot of sand has been moved—the overburden on the ballast stones."

"Gosh!" Susan said. "I never knew it was such a job!"

Her father laughed. "If you find a million dollars worth of treasure under the ballast stones, you can reconcile yourself to a certain amount of hard work, I suppose."

I still didn't know where Perry Osgood and Mr. X stood with the state, in case they were diving for treasure without a license. I asked Mr. Frost about it.

"It lines up more or less like this, Pete," he explained. "The Florida Internal Improvement Fund trustees are in charge of a lot of things in Florida, and one of them is treasure-hunting projects. The state claims a quarter share of any treasure found, as you know. It issues treasure-hunting licenses and tries to keep track of the salvage projects, and collects the state's twenty-five per cent. But the old laws about treasure-trove were pretty loosely worded and not too well enforced in Florida, so a little while ago, the state passed the Florida Antiquities Act, which replaces the old laws. This act establishes a Board of Antiquities in Florida, made up of the state's top executives, including the governor, and headed by the Director of that Internal Improvement Fund. It says the state will still get at least its twenty-five per cent of recovered treasure, but requires that all salvage operations be carried out under the immediate supervision and control of official representatives of the board, and that all treasure be valued by three professional appraisers. On the basis of their appraisal, the Board of Antiquities then decides the salvager's fair share."

"What does that make the Osgoods and Mr. X then?" I asked.

"Not criminals, I expect, even if they're diving for treasure without official supervision, Pete. On a little project like this, maybe they don't even know they're supposed to be working with the state. Briefly put, the situation is this: if anybody is recovering treasure and the state hears of it, the state does everything necessary to get its lawful share. Is that clear?"

"I guess so," I said.

Professor Harris put in his oar. "Speaking as a scientist and historian, there's a little more to it than just a twenty-five per cent cut for the state. An underwater archaeologist like me can learn a lot from sunken hulks about the details of ship's equipment and about events in the past that are not recorded in any other way. Sunken treasure ships are valuable historical documents, you might say, and the Board of Antiquities aims to see that trained experts get a chance to study them and any artifacts that may be in them, before they are simply stripped by treasure hunters interested only in gold. That's why *I'm* here tonight."

Mr. Simons rubbed a handkerchief over his bald head. He said briskly, "Well, gentlemen, that brings us back to the basic question about which we have been warily circling all evening, doesn't it? Namely, *is* there a wreck at Dolphin Inlet, and if so, *is* treasure being recovered from it?"

"It's there, sir," I said. "I'm pretty sure of that."

"Why don't you just go and ask the Osgoods?" Susan suggested.

Mr. Simons hesitated. "We-ah like to have a little more to go on than mere speculation, suspicion or rumor," he said. "It saves embarrassment all around. And it's usually conducive to so much more whole-hearted and satisfactory cooperation between the treasure hunters and the state." He paused, then turned to Mr. Frost. "I suggest that if it's possible, John, we charter a small plane at Sarta City Airport tomorrow and make at least a superficial examination from the air of the Dolphin Inlet area where Pete says the diving is taking place. If there's a wreck down there, we can perhaps spot some indication of it from the air."

"Good idea," Professor Harris said promptly. "Pete says it's shallow water. And it should be clear enough by now after the storm for our chances to be better than even."

I asked curiously, "What could you see from the air that would identify a Spanish ship down there?"

Simons said, "Nothing much except a dark patch, perhaps, roughly oval in outline and considerably darker in color than the surrounding sand. And sometimes, if you're lucky, a pattern of long shapes protruding from the oval patch—ship's cannon that haven't sunk into the floor of the ocean." Seeing my skeptical look, he added with a smile, "We fly very low, of course. Practically at wave top."

Mr. Frost left to telephone in the back room of the cottage. Everybody had another thimbleful of coffee while he was gone. When he came back, he nodded at Mr. Simons. "All set, Frank. Sarta City Airport has a charter job that will do very well for us. And a pilot who knows the Keys like the palm of his hand. Tomorrow at eleven o'clock."

"How big is the plane?" Susan asked.

"Big enough for the three of us to squeeze into it all right, according to the man I talked to. Besides the pilot, of course."

Susan's eyes turned to me and she said with considerable heat, "I object!"

Everybody looked at her in surprise. Even her mother. "You object to what?" Mr. Frost said, amused by Susan's angry tone.

"I object to your freezing Pete and me out of the best part of the Dolphin Inlet mystery, that's what! Here we are, the original discoverers of the Osgoods and the treasure ship, and you want to leave us out of the most exciting part of all! *We* ought to go in the airplane, too!"

I grinned at her spunk. I'd have given a lot to go in that plane and watch the aerial survey of Dolphin Inlet, and she knew it. I was pretty sure that she wouldn't get to first base with her objection, though.

I was right. Mr. Frost said, "Don't be childish, Susan. There's no room for you. And besides, you've taken enough chances over this business already, you and Pete. From here on, we'll handle it. That's what Mr. Simons and Professor Harris came here for."

"Yes, Susan," Mrs. Frost backed up her husband, "you and Pete have done enough."

"It isn't fair," Susan insisted. "Don't you agree with me, Pete?"

I said, "Well, I'll be just as glad to leave it to the experts, Susan. I think we're over our heads, to tell the truth. That's why we asked your father's advice."

Mr. Frost said approvingly, "Exactly."

Susan wasn't to be left out of the action as easily as that. She stood up and said in a challenging manner, "I bet you'd like to know what happens tomorrow when your plane starts circling over Dolphin Inlet, wouldn't you?"

"What do you mean?" Mr. Simons said.

"Suppose Perry Osgood and Mr. X see your plane snooping over their treasure ship and think there's a state investigator in it, maybe? Or other treasure hunters who've located the wreck and want to share in the treasure? What will they do?"

I saw what she was getting at. "She means they may try to grab whatever treasure they've already recovered from the wreck and make a run for it," I said. "Especially if they're deliberately avoiding paying the state's quarter share."

Susan nodded her head up and down so fiercely her hair jerked. "That's right! And if they *do* make a run for it, wouldn't you like to know where they've stored the treasure they've brought up? And which direction they take when they leave? And whether they go by boat or car? And stuff like that?"

"We'll be right above them . . ." Mr. Frost began.

"But you won't be able to see what's happening from up there. You'll be looking for a sunken treasure ship. Besides, what if the Osgoods and Mr. X don't run away, but decide to hide some place around the inlet until they know what your airplane is up to? Wouldn't you like to know where they'll hide?"

"I suppose," said Mr. Frost mildly, "that you're trying to tell us something, Susan."

"I am." She turned to Professor Harris and Mr. Simons. "Wouldn't you like to know the reactions of the Osgoods and Mr. X to your airplane survey? Wouldn't that help you?"

"Why, yes, I agree it might prove helpful," Mr. Simons said carefully. "The state's interests here are not clearly defined, but . . ."

"See?" Susan didn't wait for any more. "So why don't Pete and I hide in the woods while you're over the inlet and watch what happens?"

"It could be dangerous, Susan!" Mrs. Frost protested.

I had to hand it to Susan for coming up with a quickie. So I helped her out. I said, "There won't really be any possible danger that I can see, Mrs. Frost. If Susan and I stay inside the woods and don't go near the Osgoods' house or the point, nothing could happen."

Susan thanked me with her eyes. "And how about this,

Mother? I'll take a canvas and my paints so if anybody sees us, I'll claim I came to paint the inlet and the Osgood house. They gave me permission to, remember."

"W-e-l-l," Mr. Frost said. Everybody waited for his decision. Simons and Harris were hiding their amusement at Susan's persistence. "I don't suppose any harm could come of that."

Susan went over and hugged her father. "Oh, thanks, Daddy! I couldn't bear to miss the excitement!" She said to me, "How about it, Pete?"

I felt a little embarrassed. "I've got to work in the fish market as long as I'm needed. So I can't spend too much time at Dolphin Inlet. But I think I'll be able to meet you out there by the time the plane gets there and starts searching. Did you say eleven o'clock, sir?" I asked Mr. Frost.

"Yes."

"Then you'll be flying over the inlet a few minutes after. How long will it take?"

"No idea, Pete," Professor Harris said. "Not too long, though. Either we see something fairly soon, or we don't."

"I'll figure to get there about eleven, then, if I can," I said to Susan. "Okay? I'll meet you inside the woods by the beach where I took my swim."

"Okay," she said.

I thought of something else. "How will you get there? Your father will have your car at Sarta City Airport."

"I'll drop her off at the inlet on our way to the airport about ten," Mr. Frost said.

And that's how we left it. It was quite late when I got home.

13 &

THE BODY
ON THE BEACH

At ten twenty-five the next morning, the announcer's voice
came thin and rasping from my pocket-size transistor. "And
now for the local news," it said. "The body of a scuba
diver, tentatively identified as that of a Roscoe Chapin from
a nametag inside his diving suit, was discovered on the
beach at the southern end of Perdido Key this morning by
a teenage boy looking for shells. Chapin's body had evidently been washed ashore. There were empty air tanks on
his back and diving weights on his belt. The direct cause
of death was presumably drowning, police say, although
the body also exhibited severe lacerations of the left upper
arm and a depressed fracture of the skull, either of which
wounds might well have caused death in themselves. Pend-
ing a medical opinion, police are inclined to believe these
wounds may have resulted from the battering taken by the
body in the Gulf, although the possibility of foul play has
not been ruled out. Identification is not yet firm. Perdido
police ask that anyone with information about the dead
man please get in touch with them. Here's the name again:
Roscoe Chapin."

I dropped my fish knife. The big redfish I'd been work-ing on slid into the sink. I stared at the transistor radio on the edge of my cleaning board as though a coral snake had just crawled out of it, dribbling venom.

Roscoe Chapin! Dead on the beach! And still in diver's gear. Then he *had* drowned at Dolphin Inlet the day he'd taken a shot at me? He hadn't returned to the Freebooter. His car was still parked in the woods. So I was probably the last person to see him alive, wasn't I? Aiming a spear-gun at me twenty feet down in the Gulf?

My thoughts began to buzz around in my head like bees in a clover field. They didn't follow any logical pattern or make much sense but I'll say this for them: they sure came at me fast and from all directions! And most of them were questions.

If it was Roscoe Chapin's body on the beach, what had happened to him after I left him under the water? I couldn't believe that the temporary trouble he'd been in when I escaped from his speargun had been serious enough to drown him. And what was he doing down there on the bottom of the Gulf anyway, while the Osgoods and Mr. X were away from home? Taking a secret look at the Os-goods' treasure ship? Or trying to? Was that the reason? Or was he only doing a little pleasure diving in a quiet in-let? In that case, why would he deliberately shoot a spear at me, an innocent bystander? If Perry Osgood and Mr. X —or Hamilton Osgood, for that matter—had come home while Chapin was still snooping around the inlet, and sus-pected that he was spying on their treasure, they wouldn't have been too crazy about that, would they? Any more than they'd welcomed me when I went swimming in their inlet.

And what about those funny wounds on Chapin's body? Could even a heavy sea do such damage to a body in just a couple of days of playing with it? Skull fracture and a badly cut arm? I knew the answer to that one. It certainly could. Easy. And worse. Yet what if the sea *hadn't* caused the wounds? What if Chapin got them some other way? What way? I closed my eyes and tried to picture it.

Perry Osgood and Mr. X come home from their shopping in their outboard boat. They see Chapin diving in their inlet. Believing him to be a trespasser at the least, and a hijacker after their treasure at the most, they take dead aim at his swimming figure with their outboard and try to run him down. They do run him down. The prow of their metal boat bashes in his skull, their propeller slices his arm as their boat goes over him in the jumpy sea. Wouldn't that explain Chapin's wounds just as well as the police theory? Or better? Maybe.

Through the door of the fish market I heard the droning of a small airplane going by overhead. Another question suddenly flicked into my so-called mind. Namely, why hadn't Mike Sebastien filled the cops in yet on what *he* knew about the body on the beach? About Roscoe Chapin? Mike was a cop himself—half the Perdido Key force!—yet here he was begging the public over the radio for information to help the police identify the body! Mike knew Chapin was living at the Freebooter. He knew Chapin was a scuba diver . . . or at least carried diving gear in his rented car. He knew the car's license number. He knew Chapin prowled the woods around Dolphin Inlet. That ought to be plenty of leads for Mike to start on as far as Chapin was concerned! And Mike must see now that it was the *treasure* Chapin had been interested in. . . .

I got this far when I made a grab for the telephone. No one was in the market at that point except Gloria and me. I dialed police headquarters in Fiesta Village. For I suddenly realized that Mike Sebastien *didn't* know there was a treasure under Dolphin Inlet. I decided I'd better fix that oversight now.

It wasn't that easy, though. When I asked Edna Jennings, the police operator, to let me talk to Mike, she said he was out. Over in Sarta City getting the police cruiser's radio repaired. Back inside an hour. I said, "Can I talk to Sergeant Carroll, then?" If I couldn't tell Mike, I'd tell his boss. Because this wasn't just a question of a sunken treasure ship and possible dodging of a treasure-hunting license any more . . . it could involve murder, maybe. Or, anyway, something pretty bad in the police line.

"Sergeant Carroll's down at the end of the Key, looking over the place on the beach where that man's body was washed up earlier today, Pete," Miss Jennings said. "Did you hear about it on the radio just now? It's the biggest sensation Perdido's had since Vince Cosgrove crashed the secret meeting of the Key Association last summer!"

"Can't you raise Sergeant Carroll somehow?" I asked. Talk about a small town police department!

"I'm afraid not."

"Or Mike?"

"No. He called in a few minutes ago. He's doing a personal errand while the radio is being fixed."

"Oh," I said, "well . . ."

Miss Jennings must have heard something in my voice which she recognized from our kindergarten days together, because she stopped with the gossipy manner and became very businesslike. "If it's anything really urgent, Pete, I can call the sheriff's office or the state police barracks in Sarta City for you. . . ."

"It's not that urgent, thanks," I said. "Please ask Mike to call me at the fish market when he comes in, will you?"

"Surely." She hung up.

Bad luck to find both policemen unavailable at the same time. Not too important, though, I told myself. I picked the big redfish out of the sink and started in on him again. After all, Chapin was dead, the treasure ship couldn't walk away, the Osgoods and Mr. X . . .

The bombshell hit me. I grabbed the telephone and dialed the police back. My grip on the receiver was tight enough to turn my knuckles white. I said to Miss Jennings, "This is Pete Hobbs again, Miss Jennings. Things are a lot more urgent than I thought! Please ask Mike the minute he comes in—or Sergeant Carroll if he comes in first—to hotfoot it out to Dolphin Inlet right away. Tell him there's a possibility Susan Frost and I might be in bad trouble out there. And that he can find out at Dolphin Inlet everything he wants to know about that body on the beach! There's sunken Spanish treasure out there!" I threw in the last part, figuring it would get Sergeant Carroll out to the inlet on the double if he came in before Mike.

I hung up on Miss Jennings' questions about who Susan Frost was and the treasure, and looked at my watch. It was ten thirty-five. Too late. But I had to try.

I dialed the Freebooter, asked for cottage twelve. Mrs. Frost answered. I said. "Is Susan there, Mrs. Frost?" hoping against hope. "Has she left yet?"

"Why, yes," Susan's mother replied. "She left with her father and the others about three-quarters of an hour ago. They wanted to be in plenty of time at the airport. Why? What's the trouble?"

"Nothing, Mrs. Frost. Just checking to be sure she remembered." I slammed up the receiver and started for the front door of the fish market without even stopping to take off my apron. We were still empty of customers, luckily.

"What was that all about?" Gloria asked me. "And why the big rush to Dolphin Inlet? Is that where you're going?"

She knew very well it was. She'd been listening to every word I said on the phone. I gave it to her fast. "I'm going to Dolphin Inlet," I said, pushing open the screen door, "because Susan is out there alone. Within spitting distance of the Osgoods. And I think maybe the Osgoods are murderers!"

I ran outside, hopped in our pickup truck and ground the starter. The engine wouldn't catch. Savagely I bore down, pumping the gas pedal. Nothing happened. Then I saw I'd forgotten to turn on the ignition. That's how excited I was.

Don't ask me why. I just had this feeling that I ought to go out to Dolphin Inlet pronto, find Susan and warn her that we were fooling around with men who might be murderers. I wanted to get her away from there.

As I turned off Fiesta Drive onto Gulf Road I thought to myself that Susan's father had been one hundred per cent right last night . . . and Mrs. Frost, too. "Let us handle it from here in," Mr. Frost had said.

"Susan and Pete have done enough," Mrs. Frost had chimed in. Brother, I wished now I'd listened to them. And made Susan listen, too!

Not that I was really worried for fear Susan would be discovered by the Osgoods or Mr. X at the Inlet. She'd promised to stay inside the edge of the woods. Two hundred yards from the point, the Osgoods and their shack. She'd agreed not to expose herself in the open. So she would be safe. I knew that. Especially with her painting excuse as an anchor to windward if anything unexpected did happen. All the same, the idea kept nagging me that she might do something foolish on the spur of the moment. Like stepping out onto the beach to wave at her father's airplane when it came down over the inlet. I didn't think she'd do it. But she might. I couldn't tell what she might do. And I hated to think what the Osgoods and Mr. X, if they *were* killers, might do to *her* if they caught her spying. Or connected her with that circling airplane that was looking over their treasure site.

I forgot all about the treasure itself. I didn't care a bucket of chum whether the state of Florida ever got its twenty-five per cent of the goodies under Dolphin Inlet or not. What I cared about, I suddenly realized, was Susan and her safety. And a lot.

I headed north on Gulf Road at the pickup's best speed. I turned down the window beside me and stuck my head out and listened for airplane sounds. I didn't hear any. I couldn't have heard them over the racket my own truck motor was making anyway, I thought. Besides, it wasn't time for them yet.

My watch said twenty minutes to eleven. Mr. Frost, Mr. Simons and Professor Harris were supposed to take off from Sarta City airport at eleven. So what was I listening for? I still had time to get to the inlet before the plane.

Then I went as cold as a snook in frosty weather. Because suddenly I remembered that plane I'd heard fly over the fish market ten minutes ago. Could that have been Mr. Frost's chartered plane? If he and his party got to the airport early—they'd left the Freebooter almost an hour ago, Mrs. Frost had said—they could have taken off earlier than eleven. . . .

I pushed harder on the gas pedal. The only result was that the old pickup shook a little harder and groaned a little louder. No more speed. The few minutes it took me to cover the five miles to Dolphin Inlet seemed like forever. When I was still a couple of miles short, I caught a glimpse through a break in the trees of a little plane circling out over the Gulf and back again, very low, about where the mouth of Dolphin Inlet ought to be. So that answered one question.

I began praying that Susan would stay out of sight.

14 𝕊

SUSAN DISAPPEARS

I was beginning to think of those two cabbage palms on Gulf Road where Susan and I parked, as "our" cabbage palms. When I saw them coming up at me, I braked the pickup hard, swerved into the side of the road, turned off the ignition and jumped down before the truck had quite stopped under the palms.

I crossed the road at a dead run, jerking off my apron as I ran. I dropped it at the edge of the woods. Under the trees my eyes took a few seconds to adjust from bright sunlight to shadow.

When I could see all right, I plunged through the woods like a fullback trying for the first down with only a yard to go. I headed straight for the spot where I'd left my clothes the day I took a swim in the inlet. I kept looking anxiously ahead of me, hoping to see Susan. Not that I'd be able to see her until I was almost through the woods. I knew she'd be watching the inlet from the very edge of the trees. But I kept looking, anyway.

And a good thing I did, because I almost missed the easel. It had been unlimbered and set up on its long thin legs a few feet back in the trees at a spot where Susan could get a clear view of the point and the inlet. A piece of canvas board rested on the easel. The canvas was absolutely blank. That surprised me. Susan should have drawn at least a few lines on it, I thought, to make it a believable excuse for her being there.

I stopped in my tracks when I saw the easel, though. The worry and the pressure began to drain out of me at the sight of it. For it meant that Susan was here and probably all right.

I began to look for her. First along the edge of the woods bordering the beach. Then, carefully, in the vicinity of the easel with the empty canvas on it. I couldn't see her. With an uneasy churning beginning in my stomach, one by one I cased the tree trunks nearby which were thick enough to hide her from the inlet. She wasn't behind any of them.

Just beyond where I stood, the powdered-sugar beach of Dolphin Inlet shone blindingly bright in the sun. Peering out from under the trees, I could see Dolphin Point with absolutely no sign of life about it. Neither Perry Osgood nor Mr. X was anywhere in sight. Yet I could plainly hear the sound of Mr. Frost's chartered plane circling overhead, the noise of its motor first receding out into the Gulf, then coming back for another pass over Dolphin Point. I could trace its flight easily with eyes as well as ears, except when it flew directly above the woods where I was on its land-ward turns.

So where was Susan? Her easel was here, and her can-vas, too, even if she hadn't painted anything on it. So *she* should be here. Right here. And right now.

I began to move around now, careless of the noise I made, looking for her. The uneasy feeling in my stomach got worse. I spent five useless minutes searching the border of the woods for twenty-five yards in each direction from her easel, and two more looking into all the possible hiding places near the easel itself. No Susan. Something must have happened to her, then. But what? I threw caution to the winds, cupped my hands around my mouth and yelled at the top of my voice, "Susan! Susan! Are you here? Where are you?"

I was listening hard for an answer when a voice that was not Susan's said quietly behind me, "You looking for somebody, Pete?"

I whirled around. It was Perry Osgood. His big chin and no-eyebrow face didn't look any different from the time he came to our market and bought the red snappers; but somehow, his manner made me think he was wound up tighter than a watch spring. He had a couple of folded-up burlap sacks under one arm. I could smell them. They gave off a kind of dry, dusty, animal-feed smell.

For a second I was too surprised to say anything. He must have sneaked up on me through the woods, instead of coming along the open beach from his house on the point. Probably because of the airplane, I thought. And why the burlap bags? Did they have something to do with Susan, I wondered a trifle wildly.

I said with as much cheerfulness as I could scrape up, "Hi, Mr. Osgood. I'm looking for Susan Frost."

"She the girl who was with you in the sailboat last Sunday?"

"Yes, sir. She came over here this morning to paint the point and the inlet, and then she was going to do a painting of your house, the way you said she could." I pointed at Susan's blank canvas on the easel.

"Oh," he said without any change of expression. He looked at the canvas. "She didn't get very far with her painting, did she?"

"I guess not." I took the plunge. "Do you know where she is, Mr. Osgood?" My heart was slugging against my ribs so hard I was afraid he'd see my shirt front jerking with the beat. This harmless-looking guy could be a killer, I kept thinking.

He shook his head, a short, irritated shake. "What do you want with her?"

"I've got a message for her from her mother. I was making a delivery out this way, and . . ."

I didn't have time to finish my lie. Osgood interrupted me. "I guess she must have left before you got here," he said. "Too bad. Maybe you can catch up with her on Gulf Road, Pete." In other words, I thought, scram.

"If she left, she wouldn't have gone without her easel," I argued. "You sure she's not here, Mr. Osgood?"

"You can see for yourself."

The airplane came by low over our heads, hidden from us by the tree branches under which we stood. Osgood's eyes flicked upward toward the sound just once. His voice was sharper when he went on, lifted above the airplane racket, "As a matter of fact, I *told* her to leave, Pete. This is private property, you know. And it just so happens I didn't want her around today, getting underfoot. So I sent her home. The same thing goes for you. I'm busy right now. I've got no time to waste on kids. So how about getting off my property?"

He sounded anxious. And I guess he was. I asked him again, "How come Susan didn't take her painting equipment with her when she left?"

"Because I told her she could come back and paint tomorrow," Osgood said gruffly. "So she left her stuff set up."

That sounded reasonable enough to be true. It wasn't, though, I knew that. Susan wouldn't have left the inlet today, even if ordered to. She might have pretended to leave. But she wouldn't have gone far. Not when she knew I was coming to join her. Not while her father's survey plane was still overhead. She'd still be keeping tabs on the inlet. From some other vantage point, maybe, but somewhere near by. As she'd said herself, this was too exciting to miss.

I said, "Oh, well, we certainly don't want to bother you, Mr. Osgood. I'm sorry." Then I turned as though to leave. My stomach was up in my throat. I thought, what if Osgood had stumbled on Susan in the woods, just as he had me? And connected her with the strange airplane flying over the inlet? And hadn't believed her when she handed him the painting excuse? What would he have done? It gave me a fit of shivers to think about it. Because the chances were good that this old schoolmate of Pop's was capable of almost anything, up to and including murder!

Murder. That reminded me. I swung back to Perry Osgood.

"Say, Mr. Osgood," I said, "I was sorry to hear about your friend getting killed."

Osgood's arm made a sudden movement, crushing the burlap bags against his chest. "What are you talking about?" he said hoarsely.

"Your friend, Roscoe Chapin. Didn't you hear the news about him on the radio this morning?"

He didn't ask me what news. He said, "Roscoe Chapin?" and drilled me with those pale blue eyes of his.

"Yes, sir. His body was found on the beach at the south end of the Key this morning. Drowned. With a busted head and a bad cut on his arm."

Osgood's lack of reaction told me that this was stale news to him. Had he heard it over the radio himself? Or did he know that Chapin was dead because he and Mr. X had been personally responsible? I wished I knew.

His next question came very quickly. "What gave you the idea this Roger Chapin, or whoever he is, was a friend of mine?"

"Why, you told me he was, Mr. Osgood. You told me he was the friend who recommended our fish market to you. Don't you remember? When you bought the snappers?" I gave him a surprised look.

He growled, "I never heard of anybody named Roger Chapin in my life."

"Roscoe Chapin."

"Him, either. You must have misunderstood me, Pete."

I acted puzzled. "Well, that's funny," I said, "I was sure he was a friend of yours. I ran into him right here in Dolphin Inlet the other day . . . scuba diving out there by the point."

I thought that would shake him. And it did. He jumped as though I'd stuck a pin in him. "What?" he said.

"Yes, sir, he was out there just beyond the mouth of the inlet. And Susan and I have seen him hanging around here a lot."

He swallowed. "Nobody's been hanging around here, as you call it, except you nosy kids and us," he said then, angrily.

I stuck in another pin. I had to. I was desperate to find out about Susan. The airplane was making another circle over the inlet. This could be the last pass, I realized. Professor Harris had said last night that the aerial survey shouldn't take very long. So I picked Osgood up on his last remark. "Nobody except 'us,' " I repeated. "Who do you mean by 'us'?"

"My brother and I, who else?" He gave me a startled look.

I laughed. "Oh, no, not you and your brother, sir. You've got to be joking. You and the mysterious Mr. X, maybe, but not you and your brother."

He wet his lips with his tongue and if he'd had eyebrows, he'd have frowned with them. The faint trace of something that could have been fear showed on his thin face. "Mr. X? Have you lost your mind?" was all he could come up with. "Who's Mr. X?"

"That's what I call the fellow who lives here with you, Mr. Osgood," I explained to him. "The man who's posing as Hamilton Osgood, your brother."

He was ready for that one. It was his turn to laugh.

"Pete, you're a pure caution!" he said between guffaws that didn't sound quite right. "You trying to tell me you believe my brother Ham is somebody else named Mr. X?"

"That's it," I said. I remembered clearly the last line of the letter we'd found in the Osgoods' burner basket. "And what's more, Mr. Osgood, I think your brother Hamilton is dead!"

Perry Osgood went still as death himself for a split second. Then his lips curled in a half-smile. "Well, now, that's certainly an odd thought," he said. He paused long enough to shift his burlap sacks to the other arm. "Maybe you better come on up to the house right now and tell that one to my brother in person. Tell him he's dead. He'll be surprised to hear it!"

His tone was so right, his amused manner so real, that for a minute I had a sinking feeling that I was all wrong about Mr. X and Roscoe Chapin and the whole Dolphin Inlet mystery—that I was just a brash kid sticking my nose into business that didn't concern me and making a real fool of myself in the process.

But what about Susan? She had to be here still. And she had to be either hurt, dead or a prisoner or she would have shown up by now, what with my yelling and Osgood's loud laughter. And if she was a prisoner, what was the only good prison around? The Osgoods' house.

So I said, to hide my eagerness, "I thought you wanted me to leave?"

"That was before you went out of your head. Now I want you to come up to the house. I wouldn't want my brother to miss your act, Pete. It's hilarious." He wasn't laughing any more.

I hesitated like a kid who knows he's in over his head and can't figure how to back out . . . which I was. Osgood grinned and threw in the clincher. "My brother talked to your girl friend a few minutes before she left," he said. "Maybe *he* can tell you where she went."

I made up my mind. "All right," I said. "Let's go, then." I brushed past him and started for the beach a few yards away.

"Not that way." Osgood put out his free arm and stopped me. "Through the woods. It's shorter." I didn't go for that. I was sure the real reason was that Perry was suspicious of the plane, and he was afraid we'd be spotted if we went out in the open. But I didn't say anything.

We made fast time to the house on the point. Before we reached it, I heard the loud drone of Mr. Frost's airplane begin to soften a little. Soon it had faded away entirely. I'd been expecting that. But I felt awfully lonesome suddenly, all the same.

We came out of the trees at the rear of the Osgood house. Just as we walked up the slight slope to reach it, Mr. X, in what looked like a big hurry, popped around the corner from the front and went loping down the path that led to their anchorage below. He was carrying what I took to be an auxiliary can of gasoline in one hand. It looked heavy enough to be full. And his other arm was full of canned goods.

Perry Osgood hailed him. Mr. X stopped and stared at

us as we came out of the slash pines into the open. Especially at me. "What now?" he barked at Perry Osgood.

Osgood said, "It's just Pete Hobbs. The kid from the fish market. He's looking for his girl friend." He shot a warning look at Mr. X. "Also, he's got some very interesting ideas about you."

Mr. X turned to me. "What about me, Pete?" he snapped.

I was tempted to give it to him straight. "I think you and Perry Osgood killed Roscoe Chapin," was what I wanted to say. But that was no way for me to stay alive if they *were* killers. And no way to help Susan, either, if they had her.

So I said instead, "I know you aren't Hamilton Osgood, for one thing. And for another . . . " I paused long enough to let the tension build a little, "I know what you and Mr. Osgood are doing in Dolphin Inlet. You're diving for sunken Spanish treasure!"

15 ✿

I TAKE THE BAIT

All that got me for a minute was a lot of silence from Osgood and Mr. X. Their eyes shuttled back and forth from me to each other. While we were all busy saying nothing, I could hear the soft rush of the surf on the shore rocks around at the front of their house, the rattling of the palm fronds in the breeze down near their anchorage and the occasional slap of water against the wooden dock where their boats were tied up.

Mr. X recovered his powers of speech first. He didn't argue with me about the first part of my remark; I guess he didn't think it was important to them just then in the light of the second part of what I'd said. "Sunken Spanish treasure," he murmured, not like a question but like the simple repetition of a fact he'd decided to admit. "What made you come to that conclusion, Pete?"

I answered him with another question. "It's true, isn't it? You *have* found a Spanish treasure ship on the bottom of Dolphin Inlet, haven't you?"

Mr. X ignored that. He merely asked again, "What gave you that idea?"

"I'll tell you," I said, "if you'll tell me what's happened to Susan Frost."

Osgood spoke up. "I already mentioned to Pete that you'd seen her this morning."

Mr. X slowly put down the can of gasoline he was carrying. He placed his cans of tomatoes and baked beans and stuff on the path beside it. "She's all right," he said slowly. "I give you my word she is, Pete." He made a half gesture toward the old lean-to shed that was tacked onto the back of the house—the one Susan had been so keen about painting. "You can see her if you want to. In a minute."

He shut up and stared at me. I could tell that that was as much information as he was going to give out about Susan. Little as it was, it was enough to relieve my mind a lot. Because the way he said it, I couldn't help believing him. They hadn't hurt Susan. I pulled my gold doubloon out of my pocket and held it out between my fingers.

"This is what tipped me off to a treasure ship in the inlet," I said. "I found it on the undercut beach over there." I pointed to the northern shore of the inlet. "When I put the doubloon together with your constant diving and your suspicion of everybody who comes near the inlet, including me, I came up with a treasure ship. It wasn't too hard to figure out."

I thought they'd snatch my doubloon and examine it but they didn't. I put the gold piece back in my pocket.

"Who else knows about it?" Mr. X asked. "The treasure."

"If Pete knows, the girl knows," said Osgood.

"And who was in the airplane?" Mr. X said. "If you know so much, maybe you know that, too?"

I said, "One thing I *do* know is that Roscoe Chapin, the man who was found dead on the beach this morning, must have been working here with you, helping you to get up the treasure." I hoped that would take their thoughts away from the airplane. It did.

"What makes you think that?" Mr. X said.

"Because I saw him around here so much. Moving around in your woods at night. Diving in the inlet the day he drowned. And Mr. Osgood mentioned his name to me at the fish market one day as a friend of yours. . . ."

Mr. X glared at Perry Osgood. He seemed more shaken by this talk about Chapin than by my knowing about the treasure. And that figured, if he and Osgood had killed Chapin.

Mr. X's mouth tightened up, his voice got deeper, and he looked straight at me. He said, "You're perfectly correct, Pete. On all counts except that one. As you say, I'm *not* Hamilton Osgood. My name is Bascom Harter. And we *have* been diving for treasure in Dolphin Inlet." He was talking fast, as though in a great hurry to finish. "We've recovered quite a lot of it, too, incidentally."

"Where is it?" I asked.

"I'll show you in a minute. First, though, I want you to know that Roscoe Chapin was *not* working with us. He was a criminal, a blackmailer, a hijacker. He was after our treasure. He was having us watched. . . ."

"I thought he'd hired *you* to watch us, Pete," Osgood

broke in. "That's why I checked your wallet when you came swimming here."

I said, "He didn't hire me. I never spoke to the man in my life. He must have been watching you himself, if anyone was. Anyway, if he was a crook, after your treasure, I suppose you're relieved that he's dead . . . " I bit off the word. I hadn't intended to go that far.

"He deserved what he got!" Perry Osgood said savagely. "He killed my brother. In Spain." That came out in a rush before he stopped to think.

This caught me unawares. I gaped at Osgood like a nut. No wonder he had feared Chapin—and hated him—if Chapin had killed his brother. This was a pretty strong reason why Perry might have killed Chapin in return. A much stronger one than merely protecting the treasure against a hijacker.

But even so would Perry have deliberately driven a heavy boat at Chapin, helpless in the water? Killed him in cold blood? I looked at the tall, narrow-faced, weather-beaten man in front of me. His rifle-barrel eyes were boring into me. I had to admit it: he looked perfectly capable of murder. And so did bald-headed Bascom Harter, if it came to that. Suddenly I was surer than ever they were responsible for Chapin's death.

Harter snapped, "Shut up, you fool!" at Perry Osgood. Osgood got the sheepish look of a scolded kid.

"You promised I could see Susan, Mr. Harter," I said.

He nodded abruptly. "Yes. And the treasure we've recovered so far. Well, they're in the lean-to." He pointed at the ramshackle shed. "Show him, Perry."

Osgood bustled toward the shed. I followed him, willingly enough. I was pretty sure this shed was a set-up of some kind, a trap, because Osgood and Harter were obviously in a tearing rush to leave the inlet with their treasure, and they wouldn't want a witness like me running around loose while they took to their heels. Nor one like Susan, either. So if they wanted to make us *both* prisoners in their shed, it was okay with me. If Susan was unharmed, I'd give Osgood and Harter my blessing on a quick getaway. I didn't care whether they escaped or not, or kept their treasure or not. What I cared about was finding Susan.

Osgood pulled the door of the shed open and stood aside for me to go in. I said, "Susan?" and was walking through the door when a hard hand hit me in the back between my shoulder blades. Harter's hand. It gave me a stiff shove. I stumbled into the dark interior of the shed, off-balance, tripped over my own feet and went flat on my face with my head almost against the back wall.

I wasn't hurt. I jumped up and whirled around toward the door of the shed. It slammed shut and the latch clicked into place before I could reach it. A small shower of dust, knocked loose by the slamming door, rained over me. I sneezed.

It wasn't quite dark in the shed. Years of exposure to tropical sun and damp had shrunk and warped the six-inch vertical boards that formed the door until cracks showed between them. A couple of the cracks were half an inch wide. A kind of half-light came into the shed through them. It was enough to see by.

My first quick look around showed me that Susan wasn't

there. Neither was the treasure. Neither was a latch or handle of any kind on the inside of the door. The only thing in there was me, Pete Hobbs, the great detective, the believer of false promises. The dope.

I was pulling in a big breath to yell bloody murder when Harter's voice came through the cracks in the door. "Watch the kid, Perry," he said. "He could be big enough to break down that door. It's stronger than it looks, maybe, but we can't take chances. So watch him till we're set to go. His being here doesn't change anything. We'll still do it the same way. I'll finish loading the outboard. We've got to move fast."

"Okay," Osgood's voice answered. Then, "How about the loot?"

"Give me the sacks," Harter said. "I'll get that, too. Be ready to take off in ten minutes."

I peeked through one of the half-inch cracks in the door and saw Harter pick up the gasoline and canned stuff, take Osgood's burlap bags, and start down the path toward the anchorage.

16

THE GAFF

Osgood, left behind, looked dubiously at the sagging door of my shed. In a minute, he went a few yards under the slash pines and picked up a solid piece of driftwood about two feet long. He swished it through the air a couple of times before he came back with it and stood on the path right outside the shed door, not more than six feet away. I didn't like the looks of the driftwood club. Applied to my head, it ought to have about the same effect as an iron bar, I figured. I gave up the idea of trying to break down the door of the shed.

I put my lips to the widest crack and said, "Mr. Osgood. Listen. I'm not trying to keep you from getting away with your treasure. All I want to know is that Susan Frost is okay. Please, where is she? Is she all right? You haven't hurt her, have you?"

"Quiet!" Osgood said. Then, grudgingly, "She's all right. Harter told you she was."

"I'm sorry we've been a bother to you. You and Mr. Chapin and your treasure were none of our business. I know that now. I apologize for troubling you. Won't you tell me where Susan is? Please?"

Osgood hefted his club and began to slap it against the palm of his left hand. "*You* listen, Pete," he said. "We didn't want to touch the girl. And we wouldn't have touched her, except so many things were going on around here this morning that there didn't seem anything else to do when she showed up. Then *you* came sticking your nose in again, right in the middle of everything. That's why you're in that shed. But you haven't been *hurt*, and neither has your girl friend. I'm not a thug, Pete. I'm just Perry Osgood who went to school with your father. Just a normal, law-abiding citizen. We both are, Harter and I."

And probably murderers, too, I thought silently.

Osgood's voice took on the kind of noble indignation a high pressure preacher sometimes uses, as though anybody who thought he and Harter would ever step out of line ought to have his head examined. "We wouldn't *hurt* anybody, Pete. You can see that. Not even you." He got a little bitter. "Much as you deserve it! You're a rank nuisance!"

But not as much of a nuisance as Roscoe Chapin was, I thought. "I'm sorry, Mr. Osgood," I said, as humble as I could make it. "I said I was sorry. Won't you tell me where Susan is?"

He laughed, the same snorting horselaugh he'd given in the woods. At length he said, "Your girl friend is in the house behind you. In the bedroom on the other side of that shed's back wall. And she's all right. Ask her yourself if you don't believe me."

I thought he was lying again. Having some sport at my expense. I went close to the back wall of the shed and yelled "Susan!" at the top of my voice.

He wasn't lying. Faintly I heard Susan's voice come back to me through the house wall. "Is that you, Pete?" she cried. "Pete?"

"Right here, Susan! Are you all right?"

"Oh, yes, Pete. I'm locked in, but I'm okay. Are you?"

"I'm fine!" I yelled back. And I really was feeling fine now. For I knew at last that Susan was okay and that Mike Sebastien or Sergeant Carroll or Susan's father and his friends or *somebody* ought to be here very soon to put on the big rescue act. By then I hoped Osgood and Harter would be long gone with their lousy treasure. No reason why they shouldn't be. A pocketful of Spanish gold can buy a lot of fast transportation, with no questions asked, in our part of the country. And with a decent head start, I knew Osgood and Harter might never be found. But who cared?

Susan's voice reached me through the wall. "Have they got you, too, Pete?"

"I'm locked in the shed behind the house!" I felt silly yelling it all out like that while Osgood stood outside the shed door grinning and listening to every word.

"Oh, dear!" Susan called in a discouraged sort of way.

Osgood spoke through the door. "It'll only be for a little while, Pete," he said. "You won't be shut in there long. Just until Harter and I can get safe away from this blasted inlet with our treasure!"

I said, "After you've gone, how are Susan and I going to get loose?"

Through the crack, I saw him tossing his club up in the air and catching it again, one-handed, as it came down.

"Bascom Harter and I are normal, law-abiding citizens as I told you, Pete. But that don't mean we're stupid. Knowing what you do about us and Chapin and the treasure, I don't imagine you and Susan came out here this morning without telling somebody else where you were going, did you?"

I gave him an honest answer as far as it went. "I told my sister Gloria I was coming out here."

"Your sister, heh? Well, well. And how about the police, Pete? Didn't you tell them, too, maybe? And isn't there a bare possibility that Susan's mother may know where she is? And who was in that airplane just now? Could it possibly have been somebody checking on our treasure site—somebody else you've told about it?" His voice was turning nasty. I didn't answer him.

He didn't seem to notice. He went on, "Oh, I've no doubt there'll be plenty of people to let you out of this shed when we've gone, Pete." He chuckled, then added maliciously, "In fact, we're counting on it."

What did that mean? I couldn't make sense of it. I said, "When I don't show up at the fish market after lunch, Gloria may send somebody to look for me, but . . . "

Osgood cut me off. "Never mind." Faint with distance, Bascom Harter's voice floated up to us.

"I'm going to the cache, now, Perry! Get her down here!"

"Three minutes!" Osgood yelled back. Then he said in his normal voice, "Well, we're off, Pete. Hope the police—or your sister—don't take too long getting here. Because we want you to tell them something for us."

"What?" I said.

"That we took Susan Frost with us, Pete. A prisoner. A hostage. A guarantee that we'll get away with our treasure scot free." He chuckled again. "You understand now?"

I felt cold. "You're taking Susan with you?"

"Yep. Only for a little ways, Pete. We're going to tie her up somewhere in the woods along this Key. Somewhere. I won't say whether north, south, east or west. That's your problem. But somewhere on this Key. Where she'll suffer a lot from hunger and thirst unless you find her pretty soon. And I want you to tell that to your sister"—he snorted— "or the police when they come for you. By the time they've organized a search of this ten-mile island and found Susan, we'll be in Mexico."

"You can't do that!" I began. "That's kidnaping! You'll be caught! And if you hurt Susan . . . !"

"We won't hurt her unless we have to." His words were stiff with menace. He checked the outside latch of the shed door. I could see him fingering it. Then he walked up the path and disappeared around the corner of the house.

I lost a precious second wondering what to do before I backed up to the rear wall, charged across the shed and slammed into the door with my shoulder. I put everything I had into that rush and maybe a little bit more than I had. It was like crashing into a two-ton boulder with my shoulder. On T.V. and in the movies, it looks easy. The door always falls off its hinges with a splintering of wood. It wasn't that way with me. My shed door shook and groaned and gave off a mighty puff of dust, but it didn't budge. Not a board in it so much as cracked or loosened.

I tried again. With no better luck. And more pain. For a second, I thought I'd probably broken a bone or crumpled a cartilage or something. No use. The door was too much for me.

Suddenly Susan screamed. "Pete! Pete!" she cried shrilly. "He's tying me up!"

Through the house wall between us, I could hear faint sounds of a ruckus going on in there. I knew Susan wouldn't give in meekly. But what could I do to help her? I was helpless as a cow in a fenced field. I was also frantic.

Driven more by instinct than anything else, I expect, my eyes went desperately around the shed's interior, looking for a weapon, a lever, a stick, a heavy stone, anything that might give me a chance of battering my way out of there. While my eyes were looking, my hands were feeling over the rough surfaces of the plank walls of my prison. I was short of breath; I could hear my blood beat in my temples. From their contact with the walls, my hands and fingers collected several big splinters which I never knew I had until later.

As it turned out, it was the touching and not the looking that resulted in my finding the gaff. My right hand brushed down the corner where the house wall and the side wall of my shed came together. It was dark in that corner, because the daylight that seeped through the door cracks didn't reach quite that far. And I'd never have seen the rusty steel shaft of the gaff resting upright in the corner. So it was lucky I did use my hands.

When I felt the thin rod of corroded metal under my fingers, I thought it was a rod and nothing more. Maybe

a metal curtain rod like they used to make. I snatched at
it with both hands and that's when I discovered it was a
gaff. My left hand slid down to its lower end and the dull
point of the gaff hook scratched the heel of my hand. I
knew what it was, then. A surge of excitement went through
me. I blessed old Jude Skanzy, who had kept his fishing
gear in this shed, for forgetting the gaff when he sold the
place to the Osgoods. For I knew now that I could get out
of the shed.

The shaft of the gaff was less than half an inch in diame-
ter, the sharpened hook even less. It was slim enough to
slip through the widest crack in the door.

As I turned that way with the gaff in my hand, I heard
another piercing yell from Susan. She screamed, "Pete! He's
going to carry me . . . !" and then her voice was cut off as
though a wad of cotton had been stuffed into her mouth.
And maybe it had, I thought, working with terrible haste to
slide the gaff through the door crack and toward the latch
on the outside of the shed door. I couldn't see what I was
doing. I had to operate purely by guess. Starting with the
hook end of the gaff below where I judged the latch to be,
I lifted it slowly upward along the crack in my door, keeping the hook turned left toward where the protruding latch
was, and as tight as possible against the outside surface of
the door.

On my first try, I thought I'd missed the latch handle.
Wildly I was about to lower the gaff hook and try again
when I felt resistance under the hook out there. Slowly, so
as not to pull the hook loose, I raised the gaff shaft higher.

The latch clicked open. It made an amazingly loud noise.

I let out a big breath that I seemed to have been holding for an hour. I put a little pressure on the shed door and saw a crack of sunshine appear along the jamb. It was open. I was free.

As I was trying to decide the best way to use my freedom, the whole shed trembled to the slamming of the front door of the house. Heavy labored footsteps started down the path that led past my shed, and I could see in my head as clear as a blueprint what was going to happen. In a few seconds, Perry Osgood would turn the corner of the house and be in full view of the shed door. And unless I'd heard Susan wrong, he would be carrying her in his arms, or over one shoulder, carting her down to the anchorage, to the outboard motorboat in which they intended to escape, taking her with them.

There was only one thing for me to do. I did it. I pulled the gaff back inside the shed and took a good grip on it with one hand. With the other, I held the shed door almost closed so Osgood wouldn't notice the latch was sprung. I plastered my eye to a crack, watching for Osgood to come in sight down the path past my door. Then I waited, not daring to breathe or move.

17 🔹

ANOTHER SWIM
IN DOLPHIN INLET

I wasn't more than a few seconds off in my timing. Before
I could see Osgood I could hear him. His heavy footsteps
came slowly down the slanting path from the house; thud,
thud, thud. He walked on his heels. And I could hear his
heavy breathing. I had time to wonder why he was out of
breath. Had Susan put up more of a battle than he had
expected? Or did she weigh so much that he was out of
breath from carrying her? Not that I doubted which it was.
It goes to show what screwy ideas run through your mind
at a time like that.

Osgood walked into my line of vision at last. He was
maybe four yards away. He was carrying Susan in his arms.
Her wrists and ankles were tied. And there was a piece of
cloth that looked as if it might be part of an old gingham
curtain or apron tied around her head over her mouth.

At the sight of Susan being lugged down the path to the
anchorage like a box of groceries or a side of beef, I lost
my temper. I was so burned that I got a mild case of the
shakes, just waiting for the right moment to bust out of the
shed and clobber Osgood. Because that was what I wanted

to do more than anything else, suddenly—clobber Osgood for giving Susan such a hard time. I was looking forward to it. I knew it would be a pleasure, youth against middle age or not. And I knew deep down inside that I could handle Osgood as easy as he'd been able to handle Susan.

Well, it seemed like a long time but it was hardly two quick breaths until Osgood, with no more than a sidelong glance at the latch on the shed door, went by. Susan was kicking pretty lively at the time, and that may have helped to keep Osgood from noticing that the shed door latch was sprung. She was an armful for him, all right. She jerked and squirmed in his arms like a wildcat. He had all he could do to hang onto her.

When he was right opposite my door crack, I started to count his footsteps. I wanted to give him time enough to get his back toward me before I came out of the shed. One, I counted. Two. Three. And when he lifted his foot for the fourth step, I slipped out of the shed door as quietly as a mosquito landing on a powder puff. I took a couple of running steps and launched myself at his retreating back. First, though, I dropped the gaff beside the path. For some reason, I wanted to take him myself, without any rusty iron helping me.

At the last second, something must have warned him that I was behind him. He heard either a faint creaking of the shed door hinges when I shot out of my prison or the scrape of my moccasins on the path. Or maybe Susan's eyes gave it away, because she saw me coming over Osgood's shoulder. He started to turn. Susan began to squirm and struggle even harder than before.

The next thing that happened was that I landed spread-eagled on Osgood's back like a starfish on a clam shell. I gave a loud roar, and Osgood dropped Susan as if she was red hot to the touch. She rolled to one side, out of the way, and I began my joyful work on Osgood.

Without Susan to hinder him, Osgood wasn't any push-over. He had about six inches reach on me, and I'd say maybe twenty-five pounds. But he wasn't as mad as I was. Or as young, either, let's face it.

He reached around and peeled me off his back without too much trouble—because I wanted to be facing him, now that Susan wouldn't be between us. As soon as he got me around where he could belt me, he doubled up one of his big fists that looked like an oak knot, and hammered it home below my ribs on the right side. A piledriver would have felt gentle compared to it. I grunted and sucked in my breath with a hoarse gasp, and lashed out with every-thing I had. And that was the end of it as far as Osgood was concerned.

I guess I was lucky. I *know* I was. For my right-hand punch landed flush on the button of that long narrow chin of his, and he went down as though he'd run into a rifle bullet instead of a fist. The whites of his eyes showed under his half closed eyelids and he collapsed on the sandy path. He was out as cold as any mackerel in our display case at the fish market.

I couldn't believe my eyes. I knew I could take him, but I never expected I could take him with one shot like that. I was so surprised that for a split second there I toyed with the idea of taking up boxing as a career instead of shrimp-

ing. Next second, I'd found a jackknife in Osgood's pants
pocket and cut the ropes off Susan's wrists and ankles, the
cloth gag off her head. She sat up and worked her mouth
around for a spell to loosen it up, then she moaned, "Oh,
Pete!" and ran her hands back through her tangled hair.
Then she looked at Osgood and said, "Did you kill him?"
She was as surprised as I was.

"Not a chance," I said. "Are you okay?"

"Great!" she said bitterly. "Never better!"

That was good enough for me. I grabbed Osgood by one
foot and dragged him back to the shed and inside. Then I
shut the door on him and made sure the latch was tightly
closed. I thought that ought to hold him until Mike or
Susan's father arrived.

While I was locking Osgood in the shed, I said to Susan,
"How'd they get you?"

"Mr. Osgood came through the woods with some sacks
when Daddy's airplane first flew over," Susan said. "He
didn't know I was there, just sort of stumbled on me. I was
watching the inlet and didn't hear him." Susan stood up
and brushed the seat of her shorts and tucked her shirt into
her belt. "He asked me what I was doing, and I said I was
going to paint the inlet. You know, the way we planned."
She sighed deeply. "There was only one thing wrong with
my story."

"What was that?"

"I had my easel and canvas set up, very convincing,"
said Susan, "but I kind of forgot to bring my paint box
with me. I left it in the trunk of Daddy's car!"

"Ouch," I said.

"So when he invited me to come closer to the house for

a better angle to paint from, I felt I better do what he said. And then he and Mr. X locked me in the house."

"The guy's not Mr. X any more," I said, my eyes traveling over the anchorage below us and as much of the inlet beach as I could see through the stand of slash pines behind the house. "Mr. X is a man named Bascom Harter. Or so he says."

Before she could say anything to that, we heard a tremendous bellow from the direction of the beach. It was a bellow in Mr. Harter's rich voice, but a bellow all the same. I said, "Stay here, Susan," and ran through the slash pines to where I could see the whole beach below me.

Bascom Harter was setting a hot pace along the edge of the woods where the footing was firmer than on the beach itself. And he was covering distance with surprising speed for a man of his age and build.

Then I saw Mike Sebastien charge out of the woods onto the beach a couple of hundred yards behind Harter. Mike's long legs were eating up the ground, too. Harter was heading for the blind channel in which the boats were moored. And he obviously hoped Perry Osgood would meet him there with Susan and they could make good their escape in the outboard before Mike could reach them. From my elevated position, it seemed to me that Harter might make it. Mike was gaining on him by leaps and bounds but not fast enough to catch him before Harter got to the outboard.

Mike took his eyes off Harter for a minute and saw me. "Hey, Pete!" he shouted, flourishing one hand. I saw it held his service revolver. "Head him off!"

I gauged the distances and figured I just might be able to

do it. I was about fifty yards from the anchorage where the outboard was tied up, and so was Harter. Maybe he was five yards closer. Mike trailed Harter by a hundred and fifty yards; he was out of contention unless he used his gun. And I felt pretty sure Mike wouldn't start shooting. Not until he knew where Susan was, where Osgood was, and that he wouldn't hit either of them—or me—with stray bullets. Anyway, he couldn't risk taking pot shots at Harter. Not until he knew the score here in the inlet first.

So it was up to me to head off Harter.

I was still doing a slow burn over the way Harter and Osgood had meant to use Susan as a hostage. And I was pretty set up by my one-punch knockout over Osgood. So I thought, what the heck, I might as well give it a try. If I could make a clean sweep of Osgood and Harter both, I might make up, a little bit at least, for getting Susan mixed up in the mess in the first place.

While all this was going through my mind, I was already on the move. Ducking back through the pines to where Susan was sitting beside the path, I took off past her down the path for the anchorage, yelling over my shoulder to her, "Everything's okay now! The police are here!"

I had a little advantage over Bascom Harter in our race for the outboard. I was running slightly downhill. He was sprinting through sand. I wasn't sure that was going to be enough of an advantage, though, because by the time I passed Susan and headed full tilt down the path for the boats, Harter was a good fifteen yards closer than I was. Mike was still gaining on him but not fast enough.

I stretched all the muscles I have in a good try to beat

Harter to the boat. I think I could have headed him off in time, too. Except that halfway down to the dock, I lost a moccasin.

Those loose sloppy moccasins aren't the greatest for running in, and when you're pounding along a rough path, downhill, they're murder. I was reaching out with every stride to get distance and speed, and suddenly my right moccasin flew off my foot and sailed through the air ahead of me like a bird.

Running with one moccasin on and one off, I knew I wasn't going to be able to beat Harter to the dock and the outboard. I remembered that the outboard was stocked with food and gas and ready to go, and that there was no way we could follow Harter, once he got out into the inlet. Unless we could catch him in the specimen boat. I was willing to bet a bundle, though, that the engine of the specimen boat had been gimmicked by Osgood and Harter when they decided to use the outboard to escape in. They'd have taken no chances of pursuit.

I looked for Mike and saw him steaming along to my right, just rounding the inner curve of Dolphin Point and still a hundred yards away on the beach. He wasn't close enough to catch Harter. Not by a country mile. And neither was I.

I was still twenty-five yards away when Harter turned into the blind canal he and Osgood used as an anchorage. His feet made a hollow racket on the wooden planks of the dock. The outboard was riding high in the water, not two feet below the edge of the dock, and Harter headed for it like a homing pigeon. He hesitated less than a heartbeat at the shock of seeing me bearing down on him at a dead run. But right then, he must have realized how completely his whole escape plan had come apart at the seams. No Osgood in the outboard. No sacks of treasure. No Susan for a hostage. A policeman pelting along a few steps behind him. And the fish-market kid who was supposed to be safely locked in the shed chasing him across the dock like a beagle after a rabbit.

I'll say this for Bascom . . . he didn't waste any time cussing his luck. He must have taken a quick look at the situation, accepted it in an instant and acted accordingly. For he never paused when he reached the outboard. As he jumped down into it, he twitched its painter loose from the dock pole. Then he turned, balancing in the pitching boat, and set both hands against the edge of the dock. Leaning over his hands to get maximum leverage, he gave a mighty shove with them against the edge of the dock. And as his boat skittered out into Dolphin Inlet, he scrambled aft over its thwarts toward the kicker in the stern.

The tide was on the ebb and the outboard began to drift rapidly toward the center of the inlet, bouncing over the little waves. Harter bent over the motor when he reached it and began to jerk frantically at the starting cord.

He was home free. Nobody could catch him now. Not if the motor caught.

By this time I had reached the dock, and I kicked off the other moccasin as I pounded over the planks. That was all I had time to do before I took a flat running dive off the dock and felt the cool waters of Dolphin Inlet close around me once again.

18 ❧

THE TREASURE

When I came to the surface, I shook the water out of my eyes to see what direction to aim at. I gulped in a breath, got low in the water and started to swim as fast as I could toward a spot where the outgoing tide ought to place Harter's boat in about two minutes.

It was a hopeless effort, probably. I knew that. Once the outboard motor caught, Harter would be away like a racer. He'd leave me so far behind in seconds that even Tarzan couldn't catch him. He was already twenty yards from the dock and gaining headway on the strong current. But I was just stubborn enough to keep after him as long as I had any chance at all. The way I felt about him, I wanted to lay just one good punch on him, the way I had on Osgood. So I swam like crazy and kept hoping his motor would balk long enough for me to reach him.

Next time I lifted my head to gauge distance and direction, it seemed like I might get lucky twice in the same day. For the outboard motor wouldn't start. Harter was fiddling viciously with the choke and trying to brace himself in the moving boat for another hearty yank on the starting cord.

I swam harder than ever. I lashed at the surface of Dolphin Inlet like a guy trying to dig a permanent trench in the water. And I was covering distance in pretty fair style when a stutter of underwater thunder hit my eardrums. I knew what that was. The roar of an outboard motor catching, a propeller taking its first bite at the water under high acceleration. I was going to miss him after all.

That thought put a little temper into my last effort. I made a desperate stab forward with my right arm and groped blind for the boat. I ought to be within a few feet of it now, if my figuring of its drift was right. And it was. For my fingers closed over the gunwale of the boat amidships. I brought my left hand around and grabbed on with that, too. As a result, I nearly had both shoulders torn loose from their moorings. The racing motor sent the boat ahead with a strong preliminary lunge that jerked me along like a rag doll hitched to the side.

I hung on. I had the boat. And Harter was in the boat. So I wasn't about to let go. In fact, I tried a little action of my own. I pulled myself up on the side of the boat as it began to pick up speed. Then I plunged down again and yanked downward on the gunwale with my full weight and all my strength.

I had no idea whether it would do any good. But luckily, the boat hadn't got much weigh on her yet. And Harter, still standing in the stern by the kicker, wasn't the steadiest steersman in the world right then. So when I rocked his boat, I rocked his steering arm, too, and the boat slewed around sharply, throwing him off balance.

Well, what happened then was the prettiest thing I'd seen

yet in Dolphin Inlet except Susan. The gunwale I was hanging to dipped clear down below the surface. Harter made a wild grab at something to hold him topside. All he got was a handful of air. And the next thing he knew, he was splashing into the inlet with arms and legs going like a pinwheel, tilted out of his boat as neat as I'd shuck an oyster. It was beautiful.

The most beautiful part of it was that Harter started choking right away. It prevented him from outswimming me, outfighting me or outdiving me, if he'd had it in mind to try any of those things. All he could do with the mouthful of water he swallowed when I dumped him was to gag and gasp and cough and wave his arms around while I took a lifesaver's grip on him and towed him ashore to where Mike and Susan were watching it all from the dock. Harter's empty outboard boat had gone hard aground on the inlet beach near by and the beaching killed the motor.

I handed Harter up to Mike who lifted him out on the dock as easily as he'd lift a baby. Mike said, "Nice work, Pete," in a kind of surprised way.

"Thanks," I said, as I climbed out on the dock. "Arrest this guy, Mike, will you please?"

"What charge?" Mike said, grinning at me.

"Attempted kidnaping for one thing. Maybe murder for another." I turned to Susan. She was standing there crying, wiping the tears off her cheeks with the ends of her hair. "What's the matter?" I asked her. "You hurt?"

She shook her head and kept on crying. "No," she said. "Are you?"

"Not me," I said. I was breathing hard but that was all.

"I-I-I guess I'm just excited," Susan sobbed. I patted her on the back and felt stupid.

"She's all right," Mike said. "She told me about the attempted kidnaping. But whose murder? Chapin's?"

"Yeah. It's a good bet they killed Chapin, Mike. Harter and Perry Osgood together."

Mike was bewildered. "Harter? Is this Harter?" He shook the bedraggled Harter in one hand. Harter coughed up more water.

"That's Harter. The fellow Susan called Mr. X. Bascom Harter."

"Where's Osgood?"

"Locked in the shed up there." I pointed.

"I know that. I mean *Hamilton* Osgood?"

"Dead. Perry said Chapin killed his brother in Spain."

"How come?" Mike stared at me, thunderstruck.

"I don't know." I waved toward the mouth of the inlet. "Maybe something to do with the treasure ship out there on the bottom. We kind of forgot to tell you about that, Mike. Anyway, why don't you take them to jail and ask them?" I was still upset about Susan's crying.

"I will," Mike said. "It's a nice little party you've had out here this morning, I can see that. Treasure, hey? Well, well, I didn't know whether to believe your message or not, Pete. Lucky I did, though." He grinned at me, man to man, for the first time since I'd known him. "Otherwise you'd have had to haul these two to jail yourself, as well as licking them both single-handed. Come on, buddy," he growled to Harter, "let's get your partner."

They went off up the path. I patted Susan again and

pretty soon she stopped crying. "I don't know what's the matter with me," she said. "I'm not usually the nervous type." She gave me her lopsided smile.

Shepherding a now-conscious and sheepish-looking Osgood out of the shed, Mike yelled to us, "You coming?"

I yelled back we'd wait at the inlet for Susan's father. He ought to be here any minute. So Mike went off, herding Perry Osgood and Bascom Harter in front of him down the beach and toward his patrol car on Gulf Road. Osgood and Harter were handcuffed together for safety. Mike could have carried one of them under each arm if he'd wanted to, and they'd have been just as safe.

Five minutes after he'd left, Mr. Frost, Mr. Simons and Professor Harris showed up. Susan and I were sitting under the slash pines waiting for them as they walked down the beach. They had seen Mike loading his two prisoners into his cruiser on Gulf Road and were full of questions.

Mr. Frost got pretty excited himself when he heard our story, and had to be convinced over and over that Susan was really okay. Professor Harris and Mr. Simons were upset, too, but not as much as Susan's father.

When we'd told them everything that had happened to us, I asked Mr. Simons about the airplane survey. He laughed. "You were right as rain, Pete," he said. "There's a sunken ship down there on the bottom of the Gulf just outside the mouth of the inlet. From the air, we spotted a dark patch on our fifth pass, and saw long cannon shapes, and if there isn't a pile of ballast stones and decayed timbers down there from a Spanish treasure ship, I'm ready to resign my job."

"It's there," Professor Harris added. "Just as you thought, Pete."

"Harter and Osgood admitted to me they'd been diving for treasure," I said, "when they thought they could get away with some of it."

"So now we've got clear evidence of a treasure find," Simons said dryly. "And the state could collect its quarter. The only trouble is, the men who found the treasure are under arrest and the whereabouts of the treasure they've recovered is not known."

"When they see they're cooked," Mr. Frost said, "maybe they'll tell where the treasure is."

"Why should they?" asked Professor Harris. "Suppose they go to prison for kidnaping or murder or whatever. They'll get out sometime. Or one of them will. And he'll be able to go straight to a large hidden fortune that will help to compensate for his past problems. *If* they keep quiet about the treasure in the meanwhile. I wouldn't tell where the treasure is, myself, under the circumstances, would you? The ship, yes, we've located that, and can salvage anything that remains in her. But the treasure already brought up? Uh-uh. Might as well kiss your quarter share of that good-by, I'd say." He grinned at Mr. Simons.

Susan said, "I think those two sacks Mr. Osgood was carrying when he ran into me were to carry the treasure away in."

I said, "I know they were. He was carrying them when he ran into me, too. And Harter took them when he said he was going for the loot."

Simons brightened up. "Then maybe we can find it on

our own. Will you show us where you were when he surprised you in the woods?"

"Sure," I said. "I know one thing. The treasure isn't in the shed where they said it was. The dirt floor in there hasn't been disturbed for fifty years. And I guess they wouldn't hide the treasure in their house, the first place anyone would look for it. So it's got to be over there in the woods someplace between Gulf Road and the inlet beach. Probably right around the spot where I heard the whistle of warning on my first visit to the inlet. Osgood might have been making a trip to their cache when I busted in for a swim. And he whistled to Harter not far from where Susan and I met Osgood with his sacks today."

Susan jumped up. Her face was pink with excitement and sunburn. "Come on!" she said. "What are we waiting for? Let's go find the treasure!"

We all took off down the beach like kids that have just figured out where Captain Kidd buried his chest. And if you look at it in one way, we had. Susan and I led the way. We had to move fast to keep ahead of Mr. Frost, Mr. Simons and Professor Harris. They were stepping right on our heels.

We came to Susan's easel, still standing splay-legged inside the edge of the trees with the blank canvas on it. It looked lonesome now. And it seemed hours since I'd seen it the first time. "That's where I was when Mr. Osgood caught me," Susan said.

"That's where I ran into him, too," I said. "So let's turn through the woods toward Gulf Road about here." We did so. "That night Chapin followed us through the woods,"

I said to Susan, "I bet he was trying to find out the same thing we are now—where the treasure's hidden."

"Of course!" Susan said. "*That's* why he followed us in the dark. He thought maybe we were Osgood and Harter and would lead him to the treasure."

Mr. Frost said briskly, "Where were you when you heard that whistle, Pete?"

I couldn't be sure of the exact spot. After all, I'd thought it was a bird at the time, and hadn't been paying attention. Yet I felt fairly sure that I could nail the place down within fifty feet either way. The whistle had seemed to come from a tangle of underbrush to my left, I remembered, as I walked toward the inlet that first afternoon. That would put the tangle of underbrush to my right now, walking in the reverse direction. I kept my eyes peeled for it.

I passed three or four possibles on my right before I thought we were far enough into the woods. I looked over my shoulder once at Susan and the three men who were following us. I had to laugh to myself at the solemn, fired-up look on all their faces. Their eyes were squinted and their lips pressed together and they all breathed short. Talk about treasure hunters! We were a prime group, all right. I felt the pressure myself. Like when you get that first hard strike from a big sheepshead and set the hook, and wait without breathing to see whether you can play him free or whether he's going to run under a rock and snap off your hook, leader and everything. It was a thrill. I'll admit it.

"This is the place," I said, stopping finally opposite a big batch of brush about halfway through the strip of woods. "I think the whistle came from here."

"Then spread out and start searching," Mr. Simons directed. "Reconnoiter carefully. I don't think we need concern ourselves with subterranean concealment. Too difficult to hide traces of digging here. And too inconvenient for Osgood and Harter to get at frequently."

We all started out in different directions. Each one of us worked slowly outward from the central patch of brush I'd pointed out. We looked carefully at everything we came across that showed any signs of being a possible hiding place for anything at all.

It didn't take long. And as it happened, I got lucky for the third time that day. Because I was the one who wormed my way into the tangled timber, dead brush and branches of a big windfall about forty yards south of the starting place, and found the hollow tree trunk.

The butt of a huge old live oak sprouted from the ground in the middle of the windfall. It was dead and gray and stripped of bark long ago. The tree had probably been snapped off short by a hurricane or felled by a long-gone fire. Anyway, there was a branch of fresh green foliage spread across this old dead stump, and as soon as I saw it, I got a feeling it didn't belong there, that it wouldn't be there, so gracefully draped, if somebody hadn't put it there to hide something.

So I pulled the green branch aside, and sure enough, there was this big hollow place in the oak stump, about the size of a good-sized barrel. I didn't even put my hand into the opening before I called to the others. I was that sure I'd found the treasure.

They came running. And it seemed right for Mr. Simons

to be the first to put his arm into the stump. When he pulled it out again, we could see by what he held in his clenched fist that we'd found the treasure. It was a rough round ingot of heavy gold about the size and shape of an English muffin.

Well, I don't need to describe all the wonderful things we took out of that tree stump because you can see a lot of them for yourself in the state museum at Gainesville. There were a lot of doubloons like the one I found on the beach. And several more big biscuits of solid gold. There were two heavy clusters as big as your head of silver pieces of eight, all glued together into a black lump by centuries under-water. There were old-fashioned knives and forks of black-ened silver; several gold rings with rough-cut diamonds and emeralds in them; a beautiful necklace of gold links with some kind of golden demon or Aztec god or something at the end of it. And a lot more besides. Professor Harris seemed most excited about some porcelain rice bowls he said must have been made in China two hundred and fifty years ago and come halfway around the world to Mexico or Peru, only to be lost on the bottom of the sea in a sunken ship while being taken to Spain. Several of the bowls were absolutely perfect, the delicate porcelain smooth and un-cracked. They sent Professor Harris into a real state of ecstasy.

Anyway, we had the treasure. We spent a half hour or so oohing and ahing over the various items we pulled out of the tree stump. We could have spent hours—days—admir-ing them. And we would have, probably, if Mr. Frost hadn't reminded us. "It's wonderful stuff," he said, "but it's not ours. It belongs to Perry Osgood and Bascom Harter, even if they are in jail."

"Twenty-five per cent," said Mr. Simons quickly, "belongs to the state of Florida."

"What are you going to do with all this?" Susan asked.

"I'll take official charge of it," Mr. Simons said, "with you as witnesses, and put it in a safe place in Osgood's and Harter's names until we can get straightened away on things. Maybe a bank vault would be best for the present."

I looked at my watch. It was past noon. My wet clothes were almost dry on me again. I said, "Is it all right if I leave now, Mr. Simons? I've got to get back to work at the fish market. My sister will be fit to be tied. I left her there to do all the work alone."

With one accord, everybody turned around from the treasure, spread out there on the ground around the stump, and looked at me. I felt like a comic on the stage who has just said the wrong line.

"Pete," said Mr. Simons, "you go if you have to. But before you go, I want you to know how enormously appreciative of your efforts in this matter we are—the Internal Improvement Fund, the state of Florida and me, personally. Thank you."

Mr. Frost broke in, "I hate to think what might have happened to Susan if you hadn't been here today, Pete. We'll never forget it . . ."

And Susan broke in on him. She saw I was feeling embarrassed and tried to kill off the formal speeches. "It hardly seems right," she said with a laugh, "that just after you've found all this treasure you should just casually go back to cleaning fish, Pete."

I laughed, too. "Fish is my business," I said, "and I'm late to work. Treasure hunting is only a sideline with me. So I've got to go. Good-by, everybody."

They all said good-by.

"I'll see you later," I said, and took off.

19 🐬

THE CURED HAM

When Mike Sebastien came to call on Gloria at nine that night, I learned a little more about the Dolphin Inlet mystery.

Mike kissed Gloria and sat down at our kitchen table with a cup of hot coffee in front of him. Gloria, Pop and I took chairs at the table, too. Mike lit one of his brown paper cigarettes. And after the first flurry of talk about the day's events had quieted, I came out with the big question.

"*Did* Osgood and Harter kill Roscoe Chapin?" I asked Mike.

Mike breathed rank smoke and nodded. "They admitted it," he said. "On the advice of their lawyer—and once they'd learned that their treasure was safely deposited in a Sarta City bank vault waiting for the state's appraisal—they were quite willing to talk. They killed Chapin accidentally, according to their story "

"What *is* their story?" Pop asked.

"Osgood and Harter say they were heading home from Sarta City in their outboard. When they got to the entrance to Dolphin Inlet, a scuba diver suddenly came up in front of their boat. He had a speargun in his hand and the spear was pointing right at Osgood who was in the stern, running the boat. Osgood says he was sure the diver was Chapin, so he yelled to Harter on the forward thwart to duck down. At the same time, he tried to duck down flat in the boat himself. Unintentionally he jerked hard on the steering stick as he did so, and the boat swerved right into Chapin. Lying on the bottom of the boat, running blind, Osgood and Harter say they felt a bump. They ran on into the inlet, though, and didn't realize until they heard it on the radio this morning that they'd done for Chapin."

I said, "Why were they so terrified when Chapin surfaced near them? Maybe his air tanks were empty and he had to come up to breathe."

"Perry thought he was aiming to kill him, as he'd threatened to do in the note."

"So Chapin wrote the note?"

"Sure. That bit about the 'cured ham' meant Chapin would cure Perry the way he cured Hamilton if they didn't cut him in on their treasure. Kill him."

Mike took a sip of his coffee. I said, "Why were Osgood and Harter fixing to run away from the inlet this morning if they knew Chapin was dead and couldn't bother them any more?"

"They were scared. They *had* killed him, even if only accidentally. And they had good motives for his murder. So they panicked. They decided to take their treasure and clear out. Only you and Susan and that airplane all showed up at the wrong minute to dirty up their nice clean escape."

Pop knocked the ashes out of his pipe. "Pete says Chapin killed Ham Osgood in Spain. What for?"

"Because Hamilton Osgood wouldn't cut him in on the Osgood treasure. It seems that Perry and Hamilton used to prospect for Spanish gold in a half-hearted way around Florida. Took several trips to the east coast to look around after the news of the treasure ship strikes came out. They didn't find anything of course. Couple of amateurs. Then their father died and left them a few bucks. They used the money to go to Spain and search historical archives there for clues to Spanish treasure ships that had sunk in Florida waters. And in a Madrid library one day, they came across a dusty old letter written by a survivor of a treasure ship that had been sunk off Florida's west coast at a spot that sounded a lot like their own Perdido Key!

"Well, they were on top of the world, Perry says. At last they had a bona fide clue to a possible treasure. But their money was about gone. So they had to find financing before they could search for it."

Pop nodded and said, "Harter."

"That's right." Mike looked at Pop with respect. "Harter was staying at the same hotel. A retired army engineer with a pension, no ties, some knowledge of salvage, and an adventurous bent. The Osgoods had grown to like him. So they offered him a third of any treasure they recovered if he'd pay the freight for the recovery. He jumped at it."

"Where'd they meet Chapin?" I asked.

"He was staying at the same hotel, too. Another American treasure-hunter, looking for clues to sunken loot in Spain, just like the Osgoods. Only the Osgoods found one and he didn't. Hamilton Osgood foolishly boasted to him about their find. Spoke of it as a sure-fire thing. Chapin tried to cut himself in on the deal immediately. Ham refused, of course. And in the quarrel that followed, Chapin hit Ham Osgood on the head with a bottle of wine and killed him . . . and then got clean away and disappeared."

I was beginning to see the pattern now. I said, "Then Mr. Harter came home to Perdido Key with Perry Osgood and they bought the place at Dolphin Inlet to be near the treasure site."

"Right. Except they didn't buy the property at the inlet until they'd actually located the treasure ship by exploratory dives. Then Perry fronted for Harter and bought everything in the name of Osgood—property, boats and diving gear—although it was Harter's dough that paid for it all."

"What was the idea of Harter pretending to be Ham Osgood?" Gloria asked.

I answered that one myself. "So folks wouldn't know there was a stranger living at Dolphin Inlet, and get curious about him. And maybe find out about the treasure."

Mike nodded. "They'd been diving almost a year at the inlet, undisturbed, before they got that note from Roscoe Chapin telling them that he'd found them. He followed them back to America, of course, when the heat of his Spanish killing died down, to get some of their treasure if he could. Or all of it, maybe."

I said, "Why'd he write the note? Why warn them he was around?"

Mike shrugged his wide shoulders. "Who knows? To scare them into panic action of some kind, maybe, which would reveal the treasure site to him, the hiding place of the recovered loot, or even abandon everything to him by running away. That's what Perry thinks. Chapin said he'd hired spies to watch them, but he obviously didn't. He watched them himself. He took a room at the Freebooter as his base for spying operations at Dolphin Inlet. From there, he spies on Osgood and Harter diving; he locates the position of the wreck and their treasure cache; he roves around in the woods at night, checking on how much loot they've brought up each day; he even does a little scuba diving himself when Osgood and Harter are out of the way, probably to check on how much treasure might still be in the wreck, so he can decide when to raid the cache and get the maximum loot."

"That's how come Susan and I met him in the woods. And I met him underwater. But why would he *shoot* at me?" I asked.

"That's easy to figure now," Mike answered, "knowing what we do. Look, Chapin had already found some nosy strangers snooping around in the inlet woods at night, close to the treasure cache. In fact, he's even been chased by them. Now, all of a sudden, during a nice quiet dive under Dolphin Inlet when he *knows* Osgood and Harter are away from home, he runs into a strange diver down there, too close to the site of the sunken hulk to be accidental. So he deliberately tries to kill you, Pete. To eliminate another obvious competitor for the treasure. He's already killed Ham Osgood. And the second time around, murder comes easier, they tell me."

I shivered, remembering that touch of the spear point on my thigh. It could have been through my heart.

Mike put out his cigarette and finished his coffee. "I guess that covers the main points of Perry Osgood's story," he said.

Everybody was quiet for a few seconds. Then I said, "Do

you *believe* their story, Mike? Are they telling the truth, Osgood and Harter?"

Mike grinned at me. "How do I know?" he said. "The part about Ham Osgood's murder in Spain is true. We've already checked with the Madrid police by telephone and they confirm it. In Chapin's death, though, they may only be guilty of involuntary manslaughter as they claim, or they may have deliberately murdered him in cold blood. They're certainly guilty of attempted kidnaping if Susan's family wants to charge them with it. But I'm just a small town cop. All I do is catch people who are suspected of breaking the law. Somebody else has to decide whether they're guilty or not, thank goodness."

"What I want to know," said Gloria, "is who the treasure belongs to after all this?"

"I guess it still belongs to Osgood and Harter," Mike said, "license or no license, involuntary manslaughter or deliberate murder. They discovered it and they brought it up. So it belongs to them. All except what the state will take now, thanks to you, Pete."

"Has anybody told Susan about all this yet?" I asked Mike.

He winked at me. "I thought you might want to tell her yourself."

I went into the living room to telephone Susan.

20 〽

SOUVENIRS

That was Thursday night. One of Pop's crew reported sick at midnight and I had to take his place on Pop's boat. I spent the next forty-eight hours either out on the Gulf or grabbing what sleep I could between fishing trips.

I felt sort of restless and let down. Not that things were dull on Pop's boat. Once, in about twelve feet of water, we got into a school of kingfish, small ones, and we landed half a boat-load before they left us. And out near channel marker No. 69, trolling with a hand rig while Pop was hunting fish, I hooked into a thirty pound cobia that took me twenty minutes to land and made my arms feel like pieces of limp spaghetti by the time I got him to gaff. When I wasn't fishing, sleeping, or helping the crew with the nets, I spent my time thinking of Susan and whittling on a piece of driftwood.

I didn't get back to my regular spot in the fish market, cleaning and filleting, until Saturday morning—the day Susan and her folks were leaving for Tallahassee. Susan had promised she'd stop and say good-by before they took off.

It was ten o'clock on the button when she arrived. I

heard an auto horn let go outside, and Gloria said, "That's them, Pete! Go on out."

I went out. It was Susan's car, all right. I walked over to it, and leaned on the front door by the driver's side. Mr. Frost was driving. I hadn't seen him since we found the treasure cache. "Hi, Pete," he said to me. He sounded very friendly. "We wanted to say good-by and thank you again. We're on our way. Mr. Simons and Professor Harris will be around for a while until the treasure business is settled, but I've got to get back to work."

"I'm glad you stopped," I said. "I wanted to apologize for getting Susan involved in such a mess. . . ."

Mrs. Frost leaned across her husband and held out her hand. I shook it. "Don't be silly, Pete," she said. "Susan is just as much to blame as you."

Susan was in the back seat. She laughed and handed me out a stretched canvas through the window of the car. "Here's a present for you, Pete," she said. "I did it while you were out fishing the last couple of days."

I held it up and took a look at it. It was an oil painting of Dolphin Point, based on one of Susan's sketches, with the Osgoods' dilapidated shack in the foreground, vaguely seen through the stand of slash pines above the anchorage.

"Say!" I said with real admiration. "This is great, Susan!"

She jumped out of the car. "Bring it inside, Pete." she commanded. "I want to see how it looks over your cleaning tubs." She dashed into the fish market. I followed her in, lugging the painting.

Gloria was alone in the shop. As I came through the door she was saying to Susan, "Come back again, and I'll personally guarantee that my baby brother won't be a nuisance to you the next time!"

Susan said, "Pete hasn't been a nuisance! This is the best vacation I ever had."

I said, "Look what Susan painted for me, Gloria—Dolphin Point." I turned to Susan. "I'm certainly not going to hang it over the fish tubs!"

Susan's laugh came quickly. "Hang it wherever you want, Pete. It's yours."

I put down the painting and got out of my pocket the little piece of carved driftwood I'd fashioned on Pop's boat during odd minutes. It was a dolphin about two inches long, with a sharp dorsal fin shaped like the point at Dolphin Inlet, and a flat place on the back to mount a pin on. "I guess we both had the same idea," I said, and handed it to Susan. She turned it this way and that, examining it. At last she said, "Why, Pete, I didn't know you were a sculptor. Did you carve this?"

"Yeah," I said, "with a fish knife."

"For me? Is this flat place to mount a pin on?"

"Yep."

"It's beautiful." Susan closed her hand on the dolphin carving. "Thank you very much. For this . . . and everything."

Without any warning at all, Susan reached up and pulled my head down with her hands and kissed me. "Good-by, Pete," she said.

I heard her footsteps going down the front steps. A starter whirred and a motor roared outside. Then the sound of her car retreated down our sandy lane.

I sneaked a sidelong look at Gloria. She said softly, "What's the matter with you, Pete? You just stood there like a wooden Indian when she kissed you. Why didn't you kiss her back?"

I was wondering the same thing myself. But it was none of Gloria's business. I said, "You take care of your kissing, Gloria, and I'll take care of mine."

I went over to the cleaning table and picked up my knife and started on a Spanish mackerel for Mrs. Corwin's Saturday morning order.

All of a sudden I felt like a million dollars. I started to whistle.

It wasn't until an hour later that I began to worry about whether I'd smelled of fish when Susan kissed me good-by.